T0142710

Other Books By PJ Karr, Ph.D.

Epiphanies
Muses and Revelations for Mindful Connections, Re-Awakenings, and Our Harmony

2020 Archway Publishing
www.archwaypublishing.com

Spellbound
A Memoir

2019 Archway Publishing
www.archwaypublishing.com

Cliffhangers
Dramas and The Renaissance

2017 Archway Publishing
www.archwaypublishing.com

I Never Stopped...

2016 Archway Publishing
www.archwaypublishing.com

Daring Divas

2015 Archway Publishing
www.archwaypublishing.com

Tango On
Attitude = Altitude

2014 Archway Publishing
www.archwaypublishing.com

Catchin' the Sun and Moonbeams, Dad...
Play, Laugh, Love

2013 Archway Publishing
www.archwaypublishing.com

40 Ways to Stretch Your Smileage

2011 Dorrance Publishers

AHA Epiphanies to Release the Spirit Within

2009 Dorrance Publishers

Soar With a Caress of Spirit

Stories For Our Mindful Hearts

PJ Karr, Ph.D.

This is a work of fiction. All of the characters, names, incidents, organizations, and dialogue in this novel are either the products of the author's imagination or are used fictitiously.

Archway Publishing books may be ordered through booksellers or by contacting:

Archway Publishing
1663 Liberty Drive
Bloomington, IN 47403
www.archwaypublishing.com
844-669-3957

Interior Image Credit: PJ Karr, Ph.D.

ISBN: 978-1-6657-1614-7 (sc)
ISBN: 978-1-6657-1615-4 (e)

Library of Congress Control Number: 2021924858

Print information available on the last page.

Archway Publishing rev. date: 12/31/2021

Dedications

Avant-garde and compassionate Antonio…

To our authenticity of "one in another" and "equals" in the whispering winds of time…

To our promise of transformation and infusing what is possible with an imaginative spirit…

To our appreciation, a presentness, and our unconditional connection…

To our infinite bond of anticipation, euphoria, eternal bliss, and the compelling moments…

To our acceptance that playtime creates and nurtures a resonant journey of discovery, a gift beyond measure, and a joyous life balance…

To our unwavering commitment to soar to an exponential height of awareness, the positive vibration, and an intimate understanding…

Always…Namaste and Golden Abundance

Morgie, an authentic luminary of the light in our world…

To our bona fide abundance with a harmony of friendship…

To our life forces and a realm of unconditional caring…

To our acceptance of the cosmic vibrations and the strength with a raised consciousness…

To our resonance with a soul-filled, an optimistic, and an energetic connection with the intrigue of a life safari…

Radiant Light, Peace, and Prosperity

Contents

Acknowledgments

Yay, New England! Well, at least the "burbs" outside of Boston. My Yankee roots needed a PJ acknowledgment. Our illusive weeks occurred, but an early emergence of spring was touted as a gratuitous novelty.

Bostonians celebrated an earlier arrival, particularly a budding-blossoming spring. We sported the "white legs" proudly, putting on our shorts in a heartbeat.

In another homestead, my suburb in north central Texas, our springtime was also a nature acknowledgment. The flowering Bartlett and the red-tip, Fraser Photinia trees greeted us. I honored and enjoyed a tradition of two delectable gardens as my unrivaled bonus.

Nearby east Texas with the buds-to-blossoming roses and the southern hill country with the wild flowers—bluebonnets and Indian paint brush—were stunning gifts to behold.

In both homesteads, my acknowledgment of Mother Earth's nature emergence, bequeathing a breathtaking scenery of our surprises, felt smashingly good. Nature walkabouts in these different regions stimulated a rejuvenating spirit and gifted me with an inner quietude.

Today's acknowledgments enlivened with a splendid companionship. My writing awakenings, a forthcoming zest, and my creativity heightened effortlessly with Mother Nature and her unexpected gift-giving.

When I moved back to New England—the suburbs outside of Boston—another special greeting engulfed my being. My sister and I discovered the enchanting greenery, the new preservation acres, and the exquisite, beckoning rivers with the appealing brook-lined pathways.

My acknowledgment of Mother Nature was natural, like my rhythmic heartbeat. Then something else invaded our world. March of 2020 catapulted us, as our global community combatted and experienced an offbeat virus and our ever-transposing world of daily living.

I was fortunate to live in suburban Boston. There was less urgency for the mandated social distancing on my walkabouts. Experiencing our early spring at the beautiful lake inlets and those green spaces, always chock full of Mother Nature's glories, became my sustainable treasure-trove.

The mask-on visits were enjoyable, whenever we—the curious George or Georgette earthlings—paused to chat about the awe of nature. Or whenever other kindred spirits inquired.

"What are you photographing or admiring?" "Where? Oh, yes, I see!" "Oh wow, what observant eyes. Thanks for sharing!"

My appreciative spirit heightened with these small families, the couples, or the individuals, most who were without a namesake. I acknowledged this modest effort of strangers who became my new acquaintances. Our efforts sparked a cha-ching—those uplifting moments in our days and the months of our pandemic.

Acknowledgment… My gratitude became an authentic reprieve from our upside-down world. When these intermittent exchanges became reciprocal, they provided each of us with a luster of golden abundance.

There were certain days with no wayfaring walkers. No worries. I was also impassioned with my carefree friends. The PJ animal-whisperer attempts took over naturally.

For decades, my friends and significant others gave me the namesake, half in jest. Of course, they witnessed our adoring communion and my nirvana experiences.

I could never imagine not attempting my PJ animal whispers in any nature paradise. Of course, my friends were highly entertained. Yet, these divine animals deserved a special acknowledgment. These alluring creatures contributed to my beguiling and ongoing work-life balance, particularly during our global pandemic.

My close-up glimpses at the "I-see-ya" and stealthy, red fox were welcomed. A tucked-up, napping, and no-name critter with the cutest toenails made my day. Down, down, and down the embankment to my turtle treasure-trove, the twenty-one cuties, sunbathin' upon a fallen limb in the shallow waters of a lake. I was smitten and very appreciative to be healthy and navigating the steeper embankment.

Feel free to pause for a few moments. Recall a day with the bright sunbeams, instead of a rainy or a frosty-snowflake forecast. Alas, our better attitudes were evident. These surprises with Mother Nature became a PJ mainstay. The evenings with my flashback memoirs were soothing.

Nature walkabouts held another euphoria—my rustic and idyllic writing reprieves and enough grassland for my car nicknamed "Galactica Goddess." I adventured on the wanton days from my smaller, comfy condo to these outdoor reprieves. I casted the stay-at-home jargon to the wayfaring winds in these idyllic, countryside spaces.

Laptop composting happened while eating a mini-picnic in Galactica Goddess or sitting upon nearby stones and fallen tree limbs. A notepad for my scribbles or my phone for a photo and a mini-recording were super for my soundbites. They were used spontaneously with my gifted moments. A natural composting of these precious minutes or the hours could be fleshed out and cultivated that evening.

I was indebted to the front-line park rangers. They managed a local park with a lake, adding the neon signage and friendly check-ins for our safeguards during our pandemic. Week days were my favorite choice. The inviting park acreage, a shoreline beach, or the meadows became a quietude with the come-and-go visitors.

Childhood infatuation of my swimming and the yummy family picnics? Today's rejuvenation? My adult-kiddo hankering for an outdoor playtime and pure fun? Not taking today's minutes or the hours for granted as much?

Indeed, all of my questions became the true-blue confessionals. My hopeful attitude and a handful of personal intentions emerged. Plus, my manifestation for our future—the real visits and a genuine reprieve without the "new normal" at our doorsteps.

My readers or the vibrant encouragers—Marty, John of the Beamers, *Forevah* 143, Arlene and Katie Bubbles, luminous Morgie, beloved Beej, and the "open miquers" from diverse venues deserved the laurels—an ultimate blue ribbon or a bedazzling trophy. Presentness was not a buzz word, but a stellar attribute that I received from these charitable individuals.

Kudos for Josie and the skeleton staff at Archway Publishers for their support and a dogged determination. Their expertise and humaneness ensured that writers like myself were granted an opportune avenue. Our in-progress manuscript or a book finale, no matter what genre of writing, would supervene any weekly or the monthly challenges of our global pandemic.

I acknowledged my PJ bravada, regardless of the unexpected or my newest leaps. I dared to foreshadow my future writings, like a "composting garden" of lively sprouts and buds. Intrinsic and innate motivations blossomed into the spot-on vibes, landing right at the epicenter of my heart.

With this book, *Soar With A Caress of Spirit. Stories for Our Mindful Hearts,* I intended to be networking again. I reaffirmed my manifestation of another dynamite team at Archway Publishers and their professional support.

No matter what remote-work protocols would be realities, there was something brewing within my mind, body, and spirit. I needed to remain an imaginative storyteller to offset the offbeat undulations during our global pandemic.

Holding fast to my positive affirmations and taking this next plunge became a daily commitment. Remaining steadfast and stretching to evolve transformed into my heralded aspiration.

I needed to receive, accept, and refresh my daily hopes and personal aspirations. *Soar With A Caress of Spirit* was manifesting my transformative hours, the months, and my lifetime journey—with the unfolding *and* the unfinished transitions of our global pandemic.

Receive and accept,

That we leave behind the angst and not knowing,

Surrender to a stillness in the unexpected or sublime places…

Introduction

Voila! *Epiphanies: Muses and Revelations for Mindful Connections, Re-awakenings, and Our Harmony* was headed for my publisher. For two months, best couched as PJ's baby steps or a jumbo leap, an illuminating process was seized. My baby steps or that jumbo leap promised to be challenging, but did not include the unprecedented transformation.

I expected the photography changes. I anticipated a medley of the delayed emails. But, the unprecedented transformation for our world?

Our longer hours at home, the daily efforts to work remotely, and a new norm of socializing spiraled. These daily challenges morphed quickly, like our rapid heartbeats in a fierce mega-marathon.

An ever-changing reality of our COVID—19 pandemic, the mind-boggling news, and our unanticipated protocols arrived, even as we slept. We awakened each day to an uncertainty, the angst, and our months of the alien protocols.

My editorial team challenges and a series of publishing undulations with our pandemic happened overnight as well. For all of us, the real *and* surreal realms of a global pandemic were given a befitting namesake—our "new normal."

This pandemic affected countless employees, altering our off-the-Richter-scale jitters, the misgivings, or an unrelenting disquiet. Our distressful mindsets were propagating, particularly with the daily and ambiguous predictions or other skewed impressions. How did any of us juggle for any semblance of a work-life balance?

Many of us sought out a heartfelt entity for a work-life balance. Thankfully, our breaking news included the authentic stories about an array of devoted, compelling, and the humanitarian efforts.

Television anchors and online facilitators became our attentive spirits on the daily newscasts or our webinars. They became the empaths and our encouragers. They offered insights regarding our weekly stretches to conceive, fashion, and give birth to a personalized renewal and the global rejuvenations.

For my family and the endearing or new-found friends, this self-actualizing for a better work-life balance was unforgettable. Too soon, the global scenarios became historic. The forever-weeks and a colliding, month-after-month reality of our upside-down experiences and the constant pleas for a stay-connected world happened.

I made a non-negotiable commitment. Hang tight with my expressed optimism. Even with our yin and yang, I vowed to move forward daily with my new meanderings.

My turtle-like pace continued. Courage to explore, my discovery learnings, and feeling less angst permitted and nurtured my improved attitude and the helpful actions.

My intentional writing manifested a daily, proactive attitude and my intrinsic pursuits. I ventured beyond the cordial responses of my publishing protocols. So did my editorial consultant. Josie and I pursued the valued phone calls during the unpredictable months of our remote connections.

Both of us took each opportune moment to raise the bar. We included our tidbits of upbeat, whimsical, or spontaneous comments in a potpourri of emails. A whimsical or upbeat ditto occurred with my techno-attachments and a smorgasbord of my emerging software hurdles.

Josie's engaging and caring persona became an unexpected gift. I was so grateful. Our online paths intersected for reasons that I barely fathomed. But, I just knew. Permit this meaningful essence, our kindred connections with my writings and the photography, and that rare calm to abide longer in my heart.

Three days after my *Epiphanies* book submission, a familiar "PJ vibe" landed spot on. The flood gates opened with another writing endeavor. My revived, tango-on spirit received and welcomed my private reflections.

I already know. Things are really stirring again. I remember so well. Tango On: Attitude = Altitude. These earlier compositions became my book. I am still impassioned to keep on writing. Write and publish another book? Just do it!

I contemplated my reflective and seemingly telepathic moments. Touche` This start-up happened five years ago. Well, I reopened my books folder. Would a foggy memory, some clarity, or a resonant book title emerge?

I eyeballed a probable title, but did not remember a completion of my three stories. My PJ muse began to wonder about this five-years-ago companion of the heart. Hmm, my telepathic messenger, what say thee?

Yeah, we three stories are staring back from your beloved laptop and today's musings. Hey, there is already a title for each story. I bet if you read us again, there are more than foggy memories.

Surprise and surprise! Now, go forth with a PJ writing passion. Oh yeah, check out that book title. Too weird, eh?

My title was "Cloak and Dagger." Really? What was I thinking with that headliner? I laugh-snorted in a split-second and proceeded to rationalize pronto. Of course, they were my *fiction stories.*

How convenient that my new consciousness popped up simultaneously. Plus, a novel title sprang forth.

This heartfelt title percolated on May 23, 2020. I had parked my car for a nature walkabout. The quilt-like clouds and those blue-aquamarine skies were mesmerizing. Suddenly, I sensed something else.

Look upward. Towards the right side of today's skyline. Look up!

There were two hawks soaring in proximity, then flying in tandem. The hawks came closer, almost touching their beaks. Beautiful! This soaring and a mystical caress of spirit happened for fifteen minutes. Finally, the hawks soared higher, flying away into that blue-aquamarine skyline etched with the quilt-like clouds.

Today's walkabout was almost like a flashback witnessed with a former beau. Two hawks were much closer and did an amazing free-fall. We spotted their beaks touching, almost like a kiss.

Our mutual witnessing was shortly after my parents died. I even composed a nostalgic poem entitled, "Kiss of Spirits" for a prose-storytelling venue.

Today, my *new* book title was emerging with a timely, nature walkabout in the company of that awesome flashback. *Soar With A Caress of Spirit. Stories for Our Mindful Hearts.* My gifted title never changed.

How fortuitous! The Native Americans revered the hawk. In the totem of animal spirits, a hawk heightened our spiritual awareness, guiding each of us along the pathways in our life.

A moving-forward momentum, my relief donations, and a weekly intention for expanding my loving-kind and purposeful efforts continued to add to my work-life balance. My witnessing of the diverse, sentient beings occurred each week. In the meantime, our revolution-evolution of the humanitarian stories ramped up to a lofty bar.

We earthlings heard or read a daily unveiling—the darker *and* the hopeful sides of our global pandemic. Thankfully, enough of us attended to the beckoning, hopeful voices in our world.

We moved forward together, as our viral pandemic displayed its iconic meandering and its unforeseen mutations. Undoubtedly, this entirety was a foreshadowing of our lifetime lessons. I was no exception. My next lessons emerged simultaneously.

My expected completion of the additional stories for this fiction book? Put on the backburner again! A grand-finale submission of *Epiphanies* transformed into diverse publishing hurdles during our worldly transgressions. In the months ahead, our global pandemic continued its unsettling permutation.

I was mindful and resilient. My *Epiphanies* finale was going to happen, even amidst our escalating odyssey. I paused purposefully, making the "new normal" inclusions. I never altered my positiveness, the emerging epiphanies, and my hopeful chapters. Done deal!

An instant flashback happened. My ole' book title? Too weird? I mulled over this hindsight, but only for a few minutes.

I felt drawn—in the best of ways—at my real chances for an enhanced work-life balance. A passion to compose, the fabulous nature sojourns for writing, and the incredible layers of fiction to compost helped me. Greeting these PJ spurts of daily renewals along with my family and dearest friends softened several of our cliffhanger newscasts.

After a few days or a week of drama, any inner messages about my ole' book title went kaput. Too weird or spooky hit the trail or whatever. Ideas for my fiction stories and a gifted title began that inescapable and stirring day on my earlier nature walkabout.

Tune in again, PJ. Endearing or my new friends along with the neighbors were sharing their telltale signs. "We are on edge, beginning to stress again with the next-wave predictions." "Every day or week, there are mixed messages about our different vaccines and the delays." "A reality of the scary mutations haunt us and are manifesting that anxiety-rollercoaster again." "Even with the one or two-dose vaccination and the mix-match booster shot, daily living is improving, but for what length of time?"

My neighbors were still working remotely, traveling to diverse work sites, and had received the possible unemployment or the stimulus checks. The "we are hiring" and "good pay" signs appeared everywhere. Our surreal realms of life were already being lived or envisioned.

Hobbies and our innovative projects, exploring the diverse readings, and engaging in the timely, online venues or events helped to defuse our newest stressors. I took note that many individuals decided purposefully.

Be selective. Watch the encouraging television ads. Choose the programs that were comical, sustained a renewal, or offered real inspirations for a better quality of life. Pursue the personal options. The present life challenges deserved our innovative resolutions and not sinking into a darker abyss.

New cancellations of certain events, the varied state mandates during our lockdown and the re-openings, the failed businesses, escalating food shortages, and our draining relief funds continued to spiral. The naysayers tried to cast another veil of darkness.

This unrelenting and supposed darker veil? Our ego zone and a mania kept chattering about a dismal or the dire scenarios in our global pandemic. We were overstimulated to the max, harboring a distress of not knowing about our second, third, or the worst waves on our vast, ever-changing horizon.

Sprinkled in this repetitious, alien, or bizarre concoction was there something else, please? A viable or the put-in-motion options on this obscure horizon, please?

Enough? Enough mindful hearts heard, wanted, and charged ahead with the emerging options and our potential resolutions. This underlying positivity and a push-forward momentum revealed the beacons of light with our sustainable efforts to work together.

Many of us adopted the credible resolutions. There were varied re-openings, larger events and those transitions, our phenomenal leaps of faith, and the perpetual donations. These endeavors heightened our invaluable, collective consciousness.

Finally, it was an opportune time for these respectful sanctions. They opened the much-needed doors of manifesting a genuine kindness and our light-filled options.

Our enlightened attitudes, seeking a radiant light pitted against any of the veils of darkness, reigned as a higher priority. Each week was underscored with the spot-on surges of our resiliency and the ongoing, dauntless endeavors.

The next waves and our mutations happened. So did the COVID-19 vaccinations and boosters, state guidelines for the re-openings, and our long-awaited events. It was a critical and amazing timing to make our purposeful choices. I wasted no time!

Like my earlier book and its subtitle, my daily wayfaring and a paying forward became non-negotiable. My earlier subtitle was a reinforcement of our worldly re-awakening and a vibrant truth. Attitude = Altitude.

I soaked up enough of our humanitarian resolutions, reinforcing my personal quests to honor the local and national donations, sustain the random acts of kindness, and soar with a refined essence of purpose. I was very mindful of the altering, proactive actions happening in our daily world.

Together… Mindful hearts and the daily commitments were not abandoned, nor readily dismissed. No mystique as to why my earlier compositions came full circle.

My recollection of the genres, a different style of writing after my academic career, transformed into a valued keepsake. Creative nonfiction, the prose, the short stories, and my memoir writings started over a decade ago. Kindred spirits were also reading or writing for their newest work-life balance.

Written phrases, a daily journal, or our inventive stories did not disappear or diminish. They googled at us, whenever we unearthed them. Hardly a mystique, but definitely a grandiose feeling and a much-needed reprieve.

Ditto with my flashback—that ole' stash of fiction stories. They did not go vamoose, but googled right back at me. Alas, my comical and the compelling moments arrived on a perfect cue.

These compositions served as meaningful guideposts and the PJ nudges in our ever-transforming world tarnished by our incessant worries or any veil of darkness. The daily conversations or any breaking news that heralded a "never" or "always" in our future only heightened a frantic, unhealthy mindset.

Our long-awaited re-openings, transitions of ditching the face masks, and the rising percentages of vaccinations and boosters brought forth the appealing and the positive, inclusive mindsets. Newscasts of the next booster shots or the unforeseen backlash with quick alterations invaded our conscious, if not subconscious thinking.

Work-life balance, our newest choices, and a caution light appeared to be blinking out there on our vast horizon. I paid attention to my heartfelt thoughts, chock-full of real synapses and neurons to change. Real change included my brain-heart connections.

I know it is time to choose again. Caution. But, not my fears or a daily angst. Savor the moment of moments in my journey. Choose again. Now is the time…

I ramped up the proactive ventures for myself and my hopes for our world. Hope not despair. I moved away from any darker abyss or a paralysis to our healthier mind, body, and spirit connections.

I glanced at a former book, resting on my coffee table. I opened randomly, rereading my written words, especially on that no-coincidence page. Yeah, they were googling at me. My own writings were still a resonant vibration for my mindful heart.

Never say never. Invent and inspire a new genius.

Almost surreal, a murmuration with a rare flock of starlings,

Elect to rise above our worldly odds, like these soaring seagulls,

Become the co-creators of a new ebb and flow...

Windows to The Soul

Precious felt better. She smirked with her thoughts.

How do my warm fuzzies and feel-better moments happen with a wintry, full moon? There is a trifecta, a supermoon for this January, February, and March.

Precious thrust back her head and contrived the trifecta howls. The exuberant, unrestrained laughs came from a deeper abyss of her belly. The cackles and chuckles felt good. No, damn good—a boon, a godsend, and a definite sign of well-being.

Would her neighbors hear? Between the belly laughs and the amusing howling, Precious dared to reflect about the last three years.

For the first time in eons, or so it seems, I do not give a flip—about my neighbors who might hear or any full-moon superstitions. Or whatever else that use to rattle my cage for too many years.

Feeling better was new. State-of-the-art beginnings were an unprecedented feat the last three years. Tonight, Precious was aware.

She reverted to an earlier childhood pose, flinging her golden-auburn hair. When she grew longer curls last year, they became wavy and quite sexy. Precious liked her thoughts.

Hmm, my purposeful curls? I know that my speculations only take a minute. I adore these wavy curls. Yeah, they are an exquisite, golden-auburn color. More importantly, I really like my inner self.

The golden-auburn, wavy, and lengthy locks added to her gorgeous and sexy appearance. Her Aussie buddy teased Precious on the weekly phone calls.

"No worries, magnificent woman. Even at your age, you can get away with incredible stuff!" Corey touted. Precious envisioned Corey's infectious smile and sparkling eyes. They would talk again or FaceTime in a few days.

Tonight, her dimples deepened with the boisterous chuckles. Precious even laugh-snorted—something like a favorite horse that she had finally started to ride again.

She smiled broadly, like a whimsical cat, and pronounced loudly, "Why, Precious, you swanky and imposing diva!"

This evening revived a consciousness, a superior awareness and recollecting of her ultimate renewals. *Are the centuries-old, ascended yogis and yoginis proud of my renewals? Is the authentic persona of Precious FINALLY evolving?*

Precious was permitting something else to happen.

She was letting the daily thoughts ebb and flow. Precious watched them, as her caring therapist had encouraged.

"Just become an observer, Precious. Witness and release. Do not judge and get caught up in any hype of the usual thought-and-worry syndrome or an obsessive mind chatter." Precious began to witness this evening and her contemplations.

Confessions? Tonight was chock-full of her innermost reflections. There was a floating, lovely contemplation that Precious began to entertain and release. *Hmm, such a splendor. Juan has evolved into an intriguing guy.*

"*Don* Juan! How befitting!" Precious exclaimed, turning to glance at the bright moonbeam.

Both of them had joked about this acquired pseudonym that memorable evening. In spite of all the divas at the wedding reception in early September, they made an instant connection. Precious conjured up the vivid images in her mind.

Cinderella-like with a vintage banquet hall, the megafeast, and a towering cake, perfectly placed with elegant, white lights and the scattered flowers. A nostalgic band to dance to and swirl away the joyous minutes and intriguing hours.

Certain things never seemed to change. Behind the scenes, the reception party was like a soap opera. Amidst the whole shebang, the paths of Juan and Precious managed to intertwine frequently.

Precious was cognizant, more aware nowadays. Her caring therapist complimented and supported this budding perceptiveness and the evolving persona of Precious. The next illuminating confessionals arrived pronto.

Someone enters your life for a reason. Is it my powerful intention? Should I nod to the goddesses and gods? Tonight's resonance and the solace from my raucous laughter feels good. Actually, everything feels wicked good!

Tonight was the Hungry Moon of a new year. Precious was still in a grandiose mood to reflect, nestling deeper into the softer pillows on her contemporary leather sofa.

It is a destiny or my serendipity. Superb. Real or memorex? Neither or both? Juan—Don Juan—is the real deal.

Tall, lanky, and black-velvet hair. She noticed the striking, gray specks in his hair. Normally, Precious was not into hair styles, but she found herself checking out Don Juan's phenomenal hair.

Appealing and sexy. Euro-like, layered, and longer hair. What else? Probably fifty, maybe fifty-five tops. When they first spotted each other, Juan did an obvious turnabout and made his way through the crowded room. Precious felt her left eyebrow arch, especially when she looked his way and maintained their eye contact.

At fifty, she was "a looker." Even if that expression came from her ex, his friends, and her colleagues, Precious heard a ditto elsewhere for at least twenty years.

New recording, but the same sound bites: striking looks, long and exotic legs, and several compliments about being fit. Abs of steel and an energizer bunny. Avant-garde attire and a unique personality.

Tonight, Precious rattled off the yearly comments by heart. "You turn heads, especially whenever you enter or hang out at varied places." "You have a presence, an aura that is different—good different."

For fifty, Precious was frequently told she appeared younger—forty to forty-three years max. *Don* Juan's confirmation?

"I spotted you, even in a wedding crowd. You have a very unique presence."

"How so?" she quizzed, revealing an amused look and a direct gaze into his hazel eyes. That was the moment when Precious favored something else. What an amazing tranquility emanated from his eyes. Back to reviving her undeniable feelings.

Whoa, that tranquility in his eyes is definitely an unexpected moment of moments. Hmm, Juan's genuineness and my unexpected surprise...

Juan continued boldly. "I mean look at you! Don't you know? Or have been told at least a thousand times?"

These riveting moments arrived, even before they had talked throughout the evening and laughed effortlessly. And before they had danced and joked about his "*Don* Juan" pseudonym. Immediately, her thoughts jumped to a recent therapy session.

What is that expression? Ah, the word is authentic. A decade ago, I would have proclaimed that Don Juan seems authentic. But I am the empowered Precious, darn ready for the days and weeks of my unspoiled beginnings.

Let life ebb and flow, until there are obvious reasons to think otherwise. Of course, I see the daylight now. My caring therapist is cheering and smiling from afar.

That evening was a dance fever, a playtime, and there were free-flowing talks about everything. Precious and *Don* Juan danced with others, but returned to boogie, slow dance, and share their family stories. Without all the hype, they bonded with a kindred quintessence, a stirring and a beguiling connection.

Tonight, Precious was enjoying her brand-new, leather couch and the heartfelt flashbacks. Since her divorce, she had dated and experienced a few strong relationships. However, *Don* Juan let loose her caged inhibitions.

Precious felt a wee bit adolescent, but it was a nice, energizing type of invincible. She was more transparent and even felt wiser.

Precious cracked up and talked boldly. "Why, I *am* a coming-of-age woman, stronger and less vulnerable!" Back to the inner thoughts, as Precious snuggled deeper into the comfy couch.

Too spellbound or dazzled? Or just the transformations that occur at fifty-ish? No incessant worries. Let the neighborhood hear the joyous laughter and my howls.

There were long phone calls, outdoor adventures in better weather, and those wondrous dinners. They ate out or cooked together. One night club was a favorite with a mutual dance mania. Their chemistry?

"Pure lust!" her best friend declared, with a flagrant grin. Tonya was ecstatic that Precious had not blown off that wedding. She gave *Don* Juan a quality time, particularly the ongoing months for an unfolding, valued relationship.

Somewhere between then and now, Precious attended seven weddings. Her questions rambled on.

Is everyone getting married? Or married again? Whatever! Another blast from my recent past is floating into this blissful evening with my fabulous moonbeams.

Enter Robert James at wedding number four or five. The hifalutin name was a mismatch.

"Roberto, Bobby boy, or Willie, depending on who was talking to him. He was a noticeable and down-to-earth soul. What you saw was what you got!" Precious recalled aloud, quite pleased with her quick wit.

Looks like Don Juan? Not possible, but...

"Indeed, Bobby boy became someone who connected to my heart," Precious mumbled, changing her pillows to inhale the awesome aroma of her new leather couch.

I believe that the eyes reveal lotsa stuff about an individual. Suits Roberto, Bobby boy, or Willie to a T.

This wedding was smaller. Their talks were pleasant. Time apart was followed by phone calls that made a difference. His "sweetie or honey" was not contrived, more a part of the southwestern homesteads and his interesting experiences. No patronizing or platitudes came with this cowboy dude.

Both of them lived on the East coast now, but two states separated them. So much for the uncomplicated or the simple get-togethers, although they met frequently.

Tonight was another evening on her couch with flashbacks. Precious enjoyed reflecting and talking aloud. "Happily married forever—not! A divorcee," she stated.

"Nope, I shall not honor a pigeonhole labelling and our societal connotations. Makes for a *very* cluttered, life journey."

Precious had dates after her divorce. Two meaningful relationships ended mutually. Yet, after the melodrama of those seven weddings?

Don Juan and Robert James "Willie" stayed in the picture. Her inner guide or a golden moment was coming forth. She tried hard to focus, as the questions popped into her mind.

Crap! What does the golden rule book say? Text, email, call, and visit. Keep in touch. Entrust the moments. Are the in-person dynamics with these two, special men the real tell-all for me?

Eventually, the beaming Hungry Moon stopped hovering in the window frame. Her flashbacks slowed down. Precious stopped laughing and howling, giving into her wanton body. One last thought floated into her being.

Rest, just rest in the now, Precious…

Telepathic messages arrived with this full moon. Her dreams came with a universal gift. There was a unique glory, no matter was happening in the world. Nature reminded all of us—life was our gift, a celebration.

The next morning, Precious awakened to witness Mother Nature's enticing and golden-orange sunrise. She paused purposefully, sighed deeply, and sensed an inner, glorified message.

Heal, Precious. Things happen for a reason. Life is not all at once.

Don Juan, a bodacious beau and a soulful connection,

Willie dude, a nostalgic western vibe and a companionate mate,

Choices and a life-altering horizon loomed ahead for Precious...

Listening to The Wind Chimes

"Mom, you are not listening. You never say anything bad about Dad. Hey, he left us—me at nine years old *and* you! You were a younger, single Mom. No child support, no anything…" Leland rambled, for at least the hundredth time, tears welling up in his alluring, blue eyes.

"Sweetheart, we are doing ok. Nana and Grandpa are loving, supportive, and do not judge or ask the endless questions. Well, now it is just Grandpa. Nana is in a heavenly home. All I know is to go forward—you and me—and seek the new beginnings and even our challenges," Constance expressed, touching Leland's lean, right shoulder and then giving him a gentle caress.

The last five years meant an unavoidable, intermittent angst. She was one of the few women in California to pursue child support that was attached to his Dad's social security.

The legal process was designed for the illusive Dads. Leland's Dad kept moving, always to the different states and a multitude of jobs.

His Dad's purposeful meanderings meant only a slim chance for any child support. But, these legal pursuits were Constance's moving-forward choice and a quest for a few solid footprints in the sand.

Constance owned a few remnants of pain in her gut. Yet, she pursued all of the moving-forward choices. There were better and healthier days to replace a distressful week or a month without enough monies.

"Let's go for our walk near the ocean after dinner, Leland. You want to bring our drums for the beach blankets?" Constance asked softly, giving him a playful nudge in his ribs.

"Okay, Mom. Okay…" Leland muttered, heading towards his bedroom and wanting to slam the creaky door. He held back, especially during her loving-kind moments.

"Dinner in an hour, honey," Constance half-shouted, from the tiny kitchen. She knew that Leland needed to listen to the gifted musicians and write his soul-searching lyrics with his weekly playlists.

A yummy dinner and popcorn this evening would be a boost. On the eve walk, they carried the drums to the town beach, a small and private solace, not far down the narrow road.

Constance spread the blankets, patting on a spot closer to her beach blanket. Her patting gesture never failed to quiet Leland's troubled soul.

"You start the drumming. I wanna listen, close my eyes, smell the ocean mist, and then play with you," she offered, knowing that Leland needed a comforting pattern.

Leland had an extraordinary talent. Drumming, writing lyrics to his weekly music, and revealing a sensitive soul were his gifts. All of his teachers agreed that Leland was an older soul in an adolescent body.

Each year brought Leland's lifetime lessons. Nana had died, but he learned about a legacy of unconditional love from his strong and whimsical grandmother. Gramps was Leland's surrogate and perceptive Dad, right to the moment that he joined Mom in a heavenly bliss.

Constance was full of gratitude and love for her parents who owned such an unconditional love. She was also proud and joyful to be Leland's mother.

Their togetherness with these Mom and son reprieves at the ocean became a priceless memoir. Last evening at the ocean was an inner solace and a quietude for them. This morning, Constance took another sip of her aromatic coffee and began to daydream.

"Hey, Mom, I am spending a day with Eliot. He has a place to show me in La Jolla and farther up the coast. Some family connection or something," stated Leland, interrupting her reflections with a hug.

"Yeah, sure! Say hi to Eliot and hug his neck, of course," Constance teased, with a big wink.

"Yeah…" Leland replied gently, with a contagious smile. His voice trailed off as he headed upstairs to get a backpack, before he left out of the creaking, front door.

Constance set down her coffee, talking to her Dad who had entered from the back door, showing off his green tea bag with a smile. Something popped into her thoughts abruptly.

Oh, no! Did Leland overhear?

Constance was already telling her Dad that she finally might receive a support check. The lawyer located a next move to San Diego, California so he filed his Dad's social security information quickly. Leland was older, so only three years with child support would be paid.

"Unbelievable, Dad. His father's job is in San Diego, right near La Jolla. I think Leland has been trying to find his Dad," she managed to whisper, thinking that Leland still might have overheard, before shutting their creaky, front door.

Constance worried that if Leland did hear them, he would know where to go with Eliot. That evening, she fell into a restless slumber—on the old couch harboring a horde of stories.

The creaky, front door and Leland's tiptoe movements to his bedroom happened that same evening. She pretended to be asleep and peeked in the dim light. About an hour later, Constance went to her bedroom, trying to sleep away a bombardment of incessant worries.

"Morning! Hey, you got bags under your eyes. Sleep okay?" Leland asked, that concerned look coming forth.

"Sure. Hey, I am a bit older than you. Did ya have fun with Eliot?" Constance asked, trying to act nonchalant. "Oh, Grandpa is coming over to drop off his garden yummies for us."

"Nice! Hey, Eliot and I are going back next month," Leland replied, turning his back and heading upstairs to take a long shower. He paused at the stairway and looked back. "Hey Mom, make sure to give Gramps a bear hug from me. He knows that I eat every bit of his garden stuff!"

The month and counting or the anxiety? She told her Dad the updated story, anxious about what might happen if Leland and Eliot could find his father. A wiser soul responded.

"Constance, it is what it is. Neither of us knows for sure. At least Leland is showing a magnificent courage to find out a few answers for himself. Plus, Leland is taking his best buddy Eliot for the emotional support." He set down his garden goodies and walked across the living room.

"Why not?" declared Dad, opening his stealthy arms to give her a mammoth embrace. He reminded Constance that his giant hug included her Mom, always on a guardian watch.

Eliot came to visit one week later. It was his confession time for what Constance already felt in her heart.

"I know that you already know or at least suspect. Leland is going on his own to the duplex that we found. It was a side door, but no mistaking his Dad. God, his father still looks so familiar, just a bit older." Eliot paused.

"I think all of this shows how much courage resides in Leland's heart, don't you?" Eliot inquired, coming towards Constance for a reassurance, as he started to cry.

"Oh, sweet Eliot! And me? His worried, loving Mom. We are the sobbing-g-g humans-s-s," Constance managed to get out, after an emotional embrace and wiping her steady stream of tears.

"Thank heavens, Leland is not at home. He is practicing into the evening with his music buddies for a special gig in our town." Finally, Eliot and Constance shared a snack before he departed.

Leland had taken off several times, but turned around his old, used car and headed back home. Eliot kept Constance in the loop. She knew the day that Leland finally met his Dad.

"Hey, Mom. Love ya. Already had a late lunch. Gonna go and write a few lyrics," Leland mumbled. He went straight upstairs to the bedroom and closed his door.

"Yeah, go ahead. Love you, too," she replied, fighting back her tears, the flickers of fear, and the anxious leftovers.

That night in bed, Constance cried to release everything, the past *and* the present. Tears soaked the fluffy pillows and dampened her pajama top.

Down the hallway, Leland's blue eyes welled with tears, as he finished his lyrics. Finally, he fell into a deeper sleep than he ever knew. The dreamscape for listening to the wind chimes and his lyrics played on.

Listening to the wind chimes…

Searching soul, loss, and grief as mortal companions. My Dad? Abandoned me, any faithful family bonds.

Listening to the wind chimes…

Mirror images do not lie. I look like him, my soul does not. Return, my son.

Listening to the wind chimes…

Too foreign to my ears and a forgiving heart. Opened his door, only this time. My life wayfaring is now complete.

Listening to the wind chimes…

Life tapestry is rewoven, new beginnings from my darkest hole. Attachment and devotion are resonant, my loving and faithful Mom, Gramps, Eliot, and Nana in her heavenly bliss.

Listening to the wind chimes…

Travel far enough
you meet yourself

Emotive passages for Leland and Constance,

Gramps, a surrogate Dad and Nana, in a heavenly bliss,

Committed to being their keepers of the light,

Life tapestry is rewoven, new beginnings from their darkest holes...

Long-awaited travels to the Amalfi coastline for Christos,

Massive global transformations are surreal and real,

Fervent hopes for his poignant dreamscape to be the new reality...

Isle Of Capri

Christos was not debating this year. Southern Italy was a long-awaited visit. His dreams of the Amalfi coast to Sorrento, Isle of Capri, and Positano were endless.

"My Greek family is very important, but my parents and older sister have died," he confided, to his best friend, Lucas. "My sister's unexpected death with this virus happened in two days. My elderly parents had longevity, an ancient blessing from our gods and the goddesses. Now, a world pandemic shadows our weeks. I really want summer or early fall to be okay," Christos admitted, tears welling up in his expressive eyes.

"Yes! This global virus is making our past seem like a fairy tale. Maybe, how differently each of us will live for the *rest* of our lifespan," whispered Lucas, in an emotional, raspy tone.

"I shall not travel until it is permitted and safe. Who knows if our tomorrows may be numbered, Lucas. I do not want postpone my longtime passion and an overdue visit. Lucas, you remember how much I have read, talked, and dreamed about this coastal region, especially the Isle of Capri!" Christos reminded his dear friend.

"Of course, Christos, you are still passionate. We live until we die is no cliché. I never thought that I would be talking like this at a younger stage. I want my lifetime moments or my special desires now—because of a chaotic, unpredictable world and our global pandemic."

There was no social distancing for these unsurpassed friends since childhood. They lived across a hallway. They still hugged, visited, and shared meals, but followed the earliest and strict measures declared, not exclusively for Athens, but for all of Greece.

"Greece has faired better than most of Europe and the United States, even though our fragile elders represented the large numbers. Our economy was already distressed. All of us have abided by the strict sanctions. We love our family and Greece so much," revealed Christos, full of an undeniable compassion.

A few months later, there were travel opportunities. The hot, humid climate of Greece and Italy was making a dramatic change for safer travel. The plummeting numbers of people contracting the virus and the gradual re-openings already happened.

Christos settled on his plan for the southern travels down the Amalfi coast, staying in charming Sorrento. The Isle of Capri and Positano were no longer dreamscapes. The lowest number of virus cases, no lockdown, and several months of the re-openings in Italy made his dreams come to fruition.

Christo rented a simple, small apartment that was vacant for several months. The landlord, Antonio, was a family friend of his endearing Greek neighbors. Lucas was overjoyed to accompany his best friend.

Their travel plans went well. They received a warm welcome and were driven to their simple apartment. Antonio looked and acted like an endearing Italiano—curly white hair, sparkling eyes, and an array of animated gestures. Antonio patted his rotund belly from his homemade pasta, brick oven pizza, sour dough breads, and his cultivated, homemade wines.

Antonio offered immediately. He knew the best man with a boat for their Isle of Capri visits, the grottos, the majestic cliffs, and the eternal tunnel of love.

"No worry. I do! Two women. Amore!" expressed Antonio, flinging his arms and gesturing with the emotive breaths, his melodramatic sighs, and a funny chuckle.

"Grazie! Thank you, Antonio," declared Christos and Lucas, almost in unison. They looked at one another, clapped for Antonio, and laughed with a pure delight.

Sorrento was the ideal place. There were plentiful walkabouts, the outdoor and local markets, and it was located near the paradisiac Positano. Both of them spoke conversational Italian much better with the passing weeks.

"I spoke conversational Italian, Lucas. Amazing how we are advancing, being immersed in the culture and near our splendid neighbors. Back home, only a few tourists know Greek phrases, but it is a difficult language," noted Christos, turning to pause for a few seconds. Christos grinned and gave Lucas a spontaneous hug.

"I am also glad to be with you, my dearest friend. To make your precious visit and my dream come true. Ever so grateful, Christos!"

"Well, maybe we shall be beholden for the two women on tomorrow's boat trip. The Isle of Capri, the grottos, and the eternal tunnel of love. Ah, Amore!" declared Christos, revealing his elation.

Antonio was knocking at their door the next morning. All of them embraced and headed down a stunning hillside to the boats. On the dock, Antonio pointed to their handsome Giovanni, waving near his vintage boat of beauty.

"Buongiorno! Good morning! We wait. For beautiful women," expressed Giovanni, revealing a deliberate smile to Antonio.

It was not long. Two striking women, interlocked arms and slender figures, were talking as they came towards Giovanni's boat. Sofia and Greta were Italian, but they spoke English as well. Very little Greek.

They were off. The cliffs on the Isle of Capri held a bountiful beauty in today's sunshine with a nice breeze. They entered into a cliffside cavern, the amazing grotto. Giovanni was an expert at keeping his boat steady and backing out with the intermittent waves from a few boats. All of them were excited with the smaller, colorful grottos along this shoreline and the enthralling cliffs.

"Amore! There is the eternal tunnel of love," Giovanni said excitedly, pointing to the huge rocks ahead that formed an inner tunnel. "Bacio! Must kiss!"

The couples had talked, eaten assorted olives, succulent grapes, and the warm breads. They toasted with Antonio's homemade wine. And now, the beautiful kissing—in the entire tunnel of rocks— to receive a legacy of eternal love.

Lingering kisses in this tunnel… A first meeting, an engaging day, and the unexpected longer kisses became a precious bounty. The next weeks passed too quickly, as each couple met together or separately.

Crazy passion? Amore? What happened in that tunnel of love?

There was an irony. Perhaps, it was another legacy. The parents of each couple met as a chance meeting, spending weeks enjoying one another. They fell in love so fast. They were cautioned by their close and caring friends.

Their parents' beautiful unions lasted into the elder years, even with adversity and their unpredictable health concerns. Amore!

"Lucas, these compelling love stories about all of our parents? What are the odds? I do not want to live without seeing Sofia. We have a genuine caring. The distance of our separation and the unknowns of a world pandemic are ahead of us. Both of us, Lucas. Crazy, huh?"

"Greta and I felt the instant caring. Actually, I feel a bit loco with our intense feelings," confessed Lucas. He started laughing, revealing his tears of joy. Christos joined him, reaching out to embrace his dearest friend.

"Sofia and Christos. Greta and Lucas. All of us are going to keep seeing each other, remain fearless of the unknown. We shall bring hope and optimism to a higher good—for us and the world," Christos expressed, revealing his incredible passion with another embrace.

"There is something I read not too long ago. We need to remember and value certain truths, Christos. We cannot let yesterday or tomorrow take away from our daily strength, our passion, and a personal courage."

The eternal tunnel of love was spellbinding. Perhaps, it was a beginning of another legacy? Christos and Lucas stared at each other.

Amore…

Sofia and Christos. Greta and Lucas.

Remaining fearless guardians of the unknown,

Seizing today's strength, a passion, and the courage...

New Circadian Rhythm

Will I struggle again? Will I dare to search? What is my sacred journey? He closed the book that ended with these three questions. On top of the nightstand, nearby his reading lamp, was an ideal spot for another rereading.

Royce Parsons-Amoroso reflected, climbing slowly into the empty, canopy bed. He spoke in a gentle cadence.

"Alone now... But, I am not lonely. Will hope and another unconditional love recapture a free will and my next choices?"

Royce Parsons-Amoroso paused intentionally. It was a flawless timing. He knew to pick up a royal blue journal near his reading lamp and to scribe his honest feelings in these moments.

My pen moves rapidly across this page. I write to release any incessant worries, a noticeable distress, and my leftover angst to a higher realm beyond our earthly world. I do believe the centuries of spirituality and the archangels soothe all of us—with the loving-kind energy.

Royce glanced at a bold-print flyer from a holistic workshop, tucked in a page with this next journaling. There was a resonant question of our lifetime passages with a different peak or an undulating valley in bold print. **Will I let my free spirit start to bud again?**

Royce Parsons-Amoroso rolled over in the bed, reaffirming his solitary presence. He whispered lovingly to his pillow.

"Alone now, Royce... But, there is a readiness with my intrinsic and wanton desires to risk and to regain the ultimate joy."

Do I dare to risk again? Do I make enough space for my next journey of illuminating footprints? It seemed like Royce's heart was asking these questions, filling and enfolding his searching soul.

Royce Parsons-Amoroso rested in silence. Then he rolled over again to pen a last journal entry, before succumbing to his closing eyelids.

Royce's rest and peace enticed the new dreamscape. Tomorrow, there would be an imprinting for his next journal entry.

In the morning, the sun peeked through his curtains. Royce felt compelled to pen his awakening thoughts.

I want a new ebb and flow in my life transitions and the unfolding chapters. Acceptance. Last evening...my dream becomes my new circadian rhythm.

"Aspire to inspire
before we expire"

A vintage lodge and cozy cabins nestled into the peaceful pines,

A quaint harbor, the sunsets, and nearby islands cultivated the appreciative spirit,

Each sibling treasured the passing seasons, unsurpassed family adventures, and the envisioned partners...

Siblings

They were nicknamed the "feisty five," the three boys and the two girls. Summer and early fall were delightful at Meredith Lake. Their parents inherited a vintage lodge with a few cabins overlooking the quaint harbor. They managed well, especially with the returning families and a word-of-mouth support.

Their children cleaned cozy cottages and the rooms in the lodge. Weekly chores were rarely an issue, but the sibling rebuttals happened. Not for long, as each of them adored Meredith Lake, plus the old or new friends that returned each summer or throughout the early fall.

Potential beaus or the promising girlfriends? "It is a brand-new summer. Never say never!" was David and Jane's favorite motto. They played matchmaker for one another, without any of the wistful guarantees.

David, the eldest son, and Jane, the middle daughter, were the siblings that several families got to know across the years. If desired, the guests enjoyed a smaller speed boat and the sailboats or secured a boat-dock privilege near their vintage boathouse. The family owned a few canoes, a smaller catamaran, and three kayaks to rent.

"Hey, I need your help down at the dock, Jane. Take off those air buds," David shouted, as he motioned with his stealthy, russet-bronze arm.

"I am coming. Just *one* song, please. I *have* to text my friends, David!" Jane repeated with a playful tone, when she finally strolled down to the dockside.

"Chill out for an hour. Your just-one-more thing can wait. The universe does wait, believe it or not," David offered, displaying a contagious grin with his stellar dimples that Jane had wanted forever.

"You are a real weirdo, my *eldest* brother!"

They enjoyed the banter, got the dock chores done in an hour, and headed back to the lodge to lounge in the rocking chairs. Rocking on the porch with an awesome view of the harbor and nearby mountain range was a beloved pastime.

"Hello? Hello! Is anybody in a rocking chair?" bellowed a familiar voice from the screen-door entry.

Ah, the Flints arrived! David and Jane gave a thumbs-up sign and sported their slapstick and humdinger faces. Television kept these two millennials aware and the consummate, irresistible comedians.

"Welcome back to Meredith Lake. Look out! We have been waiting for you to arrive. Did you bring your Grandpa's boat?" asked David, getting up from his rocker to give the Flints their anticipated hugs.

"Yeah, we did. Grandpa got a new Mercury motor. He sounds like both of you with your jive talk—upgraded," Jose chuckled. He was never with the Flints in the prior summers, as he enjoyed the summer camps in Vermont.

It did not take long, as they were begging to go swimming, take a wild boat ride, and gawk at the cottage. Early afternoon was the check-in for these longtime renters.

The new folks enjoyed a guided tour in the late afternoon along with the snippets about the top notch highlights. As the week progressed, there would be fantastic cookouts, lots of swimming, and cool music to dance 'round and 'round the picnic tables.

"Yo, David. Earth to David. New arrivals with the Flints! Did ya check out Ms. Cool and her hunk of a brother? I guess she went to summer camps as well. They are our ages. Put in a good word for me? You know his sister will be curious or smitten, maybe moreso with your pics on my phone. None of the videos, I promise," Jane retorted, especially when David raised an eyebrow.

"Here we go again, Jane. I must admit, Ms. Cool is a looker. Think she will *adore* my contagious smile and huge dimples even more than you?" David teased. They laughed for several minutes, hanging onto their good-aching bellies.

Come to find out, the cookout held the real surprise. Their imaginations were elevated when they learned that their parents rented a cottage for the entire month of July. David and Jane quickly let their siblings know—keep your distance.

David and Sabrina became an item. Jane and Jose, who was adopted as an infant, became the best buddies. By the end of July, David already was planning to visit Sabrina back home. Where did this summer and the fall weekends disappear? Suddenly, the family was winterizing the vintage lodge and the cozy cottages.

"Sabrina, I want you to come to my prom," David managed to say, between their kisses and longer reprieves at the small island that summer.

"David, I am so ready—for everything with you."

Three years later, they were the high school sweethearts who married. They had the same outlook—let the universe take its course. When they started their family, Jane and Jose had split.

They had been best buddies, budding romantics, and then things went kaput. David and Sabrina never asked, but believed the ebb and flow of the world would let them know—in time.

"David, my brother's adoption was wonderful. Now? I sense that he wants to search for his biological parents. My parents are in sync with his passion, feeling it is the natural ebb and flow of his adoptive roots. I hope that he is not rejected by either parent. Hope floats, huh?" she asked David, revealing her compassionate soul.

"Sabrina, my loving partner. Let's be there for Jose. Send out light for our hopes and an optimism regarding those caring parents," David intoned in his gentle voice, holding Sabrina in a lingering embrace.

Jose had the tugs of war with his ego chatter and a yearning heart for years. Some days, he harbored an angst about his uncaring or rejecting parents, if he ever found them. The next week, his heart was full of hope and the courageous plans.

It was years. He missed a call from Jane. There was no voicemail.

Breathing deeply and closing her eyes, Jane called back the next day. She was already thinking about the voicemail.

Leave a voicemail, Jane. What I have to say is important and comforting to Jose. It means something for me, something that I have been ignoring for years.

Jose saw her name pop up. "Hello?"

"Jose, this is Jane. *Please* do not hang up. Are you still on the phone?" Jane managed to inquire, the slight tremors in her voice.

"Yeah, Jane."

"I know we split up, but I am calling because David and Sabrina shared what you are doing. Do not be mad at any of us. We care and want the best for you, Jose. Look, I called to tell you a story about a young woman who seemed so confident, such an extrovert, and had relationships. Deep inside, she felt so lost as the middle child in a bigger family. Even her brother, very close to her, did not know. Then she met this guy that cared, but kept her at a distance. Well, best buddies and a short romance. They split. Old, disturbing feelings came back—a flashback-feeling of being lost as a middle child. Jose, that woman? That was me. I just wanted you to know that feeling lost in life sometimes is for a good reason—to push us forward. If you want to talk, I can be your buddy," Jane managed to say, getting out everything and speaking so quickly that she was out of breath.

"Jane, my heart is full right now. I know you are coming from a good place with the fine intentions. I am just—a mess. My emotions go back and forth because of the imagined outcomes, if I ever find them. I need to search. Overdue for me. When I get my head and heart in sync, perhaps I can call? Jose asked, his voice so low that Jane had to focus to hear.

"Of course! Just remember us as best buddies—more than our short romance, Jose."

"Okay, Jane. Thanks."

She sat in her parked car near the Meredith Lake. Her thoughts were rushing through her mind, body, and soul.

I travel here to Meredith Lake, just so I have the courage to call again. Yes, I needed to travel here for my real courage. Yay, I finally called Jose. I am also moving forward with my feeling-lost abyss as the middle child. I am finding that verve! Baby steps forward, not backward.

Jose found out that his biological father died five years ago. His biological mother had been divorced from his father for ten years. She finally agreed to see Jose, but only for a coffee at a diner that he had to locate. Ironically, the diner was located in a town near Meredith Lake.

Jane, Sabrina, and David had his back. Everything still felt surreal. But, Jose travelled in his jeep to the diner and kept repeating, "hope *not* my despair" the entire way.

Small place. Only two cars were parked. Her choice. Now, the guts to open that door and go inside. His heart felt surreal and upside-down. The entry door had a damn bell, underscoring his arrival. There was no exiting—at least in the next few minutes.

"Hi hon, I'll be with you in a jiff. Hon, sit wherever you want," the waitress said, exuding a cute, drawling voice. Jose walked at least a hundred miles towards a woman in the last booth, her back to the entry door.

"Excuse me, but are you..." Jose stopped talking and stared in disbelief.

This woman looked exactly like a mirror image of himself—eyes, lips, nose, skin tone, hair color, and now, her exact way of staring.

"Please sit, Jose. I am Valentina. Everyone has a story..." Her message was interrupted by the arrival of the two coffees that Valentina already ordered.

Valentina began again. "I dreaded today, actually every day of my pregnancy. My family kept saying, 'too young to be parents.' Then the shocker—you have to get an abortion. End of one horror. My former husband, your biological Dad and I, ran away. Later, we ended up at an adoption agency, very frightened adolescents. Our baby would be on a supposed lovely journey into a different world, not our upside-down world." Valentina paused briefly, tears welling up in her eyes.

"Reassurance? Jose, you would have a better chance in life with a caring family and the financially secure parents. Plus, a darling sister who really wanted a brother. My gut is wrenching now... Like it was yesterday, Jose. Every year was an inner struggle, not ever knowing your story and this adoptive family. Here you are! My gut is upside-down. Your father and I divorced, not so nicely due to my inner struggles and frequent depression. Perhaps, it was your father really not being in love, just in lust and overwhelmed from the start. His family would never approve or accept an abortion. Guilt and hope are hard to mix together, Jose."

Jose had not touched his coffee. Valentina took a slow sip before she dared to stare at Jose's face. The tears had streamed down his cheeks and neck, dampening his light blue collar.

"You spoke my exact words, an upside-down world. You have to know that my adoptive parents and sister are beautiful and giving people. Over the years, stuff kept bubbling up to the surface. I guess every adoptive child or adult wants to know the answers? I am a grown man, successful, and then my world evolves with this increasing angst and turning upside-down. Messy. Very messy. So, I do not know where to begin with all of our moments today. Do you?" Jose murmured, unable to repress the obvious tremors in his voice.

"Well, both of us own a courage…with our wrenching guts and an upside-down world. Maybe we own hope? More than either of us realized? New beginnings, Jose…" Valentina shared in half-whispers and half-laughs, surprised at her emerging courage in today's unexpected moments.

"New beginnings? They were never imagined. Just all the dark stuff that goes with rejections or not finding your biological parents. Lost…and found. New beginnings, Mom," Jose replied softly, sliding his cup slowly to click Valentina's coffee mug.

Upside-down world of resisting and searching for parental ties,

Imaginative flights of fancy vying against Jose's darkened passages,

Hope pitted against the potential losses. Conquer from within....

Dementia transforming to an insidious Alzheimer's mutation quickly,

Smitten Joseph visited like clockwork, held Natasha's soft hand,

Pure acceptance of each day...

Smitten

The dementia settled in quickly. She ended up in the severe Alzheimer's unit for seven years. He visited like clockwork.

"Hi, sweetie," Joseph crooned, holding her soft hand. "Natasha, you are taking a nap after lunch, eh?"

"Hmm, a nap," Natasha murmured, without that vacant stare for fifteen minutes. Her petite hand, still with a simple wedding band, gave Joseph the tiny squeezes.

"She knew for those minutes," Joseph would always tell Jack, Janice, and Janie. "She was definitely smitten."

Smitten and married at twenty. Fifty years later, still married and dubbed "the soul-mates." That expression was a new lingo for them.

"Lovers who were *still* smitten," Joseph and Natasha would declare, almost in unison, to their family and close friends. Everyone would watch their forthcoming grins, a smooch, and the caress.

"Whoa down, the soul mates are on fire!" Jack, the eldest child, loved to tease them. His two sisters, the twins named Janice and Janie, would crack up. Friends would hoot and clap, whenever they were visiting. What a troupe of characters.

Joseph and Natasha wanted a family, casting the ultimate love to the next generation. Of course, the caring boundaries were present. But, they wanted to share the unleashed funnies with their kiddos, now the intriguing grown-ups. Meanwhile, the lofty parental plans of traveling in the United States were known. They were quick to reiterate, "Only after you kiddos were educated."

The kiddos adored their parental generosity. They kicked in the dinero, not exactly megabucks, from their adventuresome or the mesa-mesa summer jobs. Each of them overcame personal road blocks, determined to create an impassioned and promising career path.

Jack was the exotic carpenter whose home business was flourishing, thanks to his longtime partner's expertise and creative vibe to sustain an impressive website. Nowadays, there were increased online sales. Both of them attended and enjoyed the regional fairs or a grand festival for an innovative display and the potential sales. Their passion to educate or talk about Jack's artful and customized woodwork was obvious.

Janice and Janie? Both seasoned nurses in San Diego. Not married, but loved to tell-all, especially the dating-duos tales. Singles meet-up groups, the dance venues, and the online "potential dates, but no more weirdos" were pursued. Exceptional nurses, but they were never too busy for dating.

Their worlds changed with Natasha's sneak-up dementia. Next whammy on everyone's horizon? That lightning-bolt strike, sending Natasha straight to a severe Alzheimer's unit.

"Jack, do you realize how long Dad spends there? He visits in terrible weather, the late morning and mid-afternoon, and at least three evenings. Dad takes Natasha to music and other activities in the main room. Janice and I are worried about him. Certain days, we intersect with our visits. Dad looks *so* tired."

"Janie, do you think that we are *really* going to change Dad? He loves Mom too much. I bring him to our home and the studio. We cook and share healthy meals. BUT…Dad is not going to live with any of us anytime soon, as long as he calls the shots," reminded Jack, trying the best to soothe his sister and himself in the same moment.

Hundreds of talks, like this one on their phones and during a lunch or a coffee break, ensued each month. Always on the same page—Jack, Janice, and Janie would think aloud and discuss a growing angst about their Dad.

Joseph was a man who remained smitten, determined to hang out with Natasha. For several years, the nurses and the assigned caretakers repeated kindly that it was the end of visiting until tomorrow.

No one foreshadowed the "something uncontrollable" for their family. And, certainly, not for the families across the globe that were traumatized.

"Janie, I am working double shifts. This virus is out of control here…and, everywhere on the breaking news. They added both of us to the crisis-emergency team. Did you get that call?" Janice asked, literally running out of breath.

"My God, Janice. I did not get that call. Or yet. Is Dad still at Jack's home?"

"Yes! The staff at the Alzheimer's facility is saying that Dad might not able to see Mom at all! God, he is coming up with ways to visit Natasha that are crazy. Or maybe, not so crazy?"

The upside-down world that affected Italy a few months ago was spiraling into places across the United States. Breaking news happened every day.

More lockdowns, the social distancing, and the stay-home and work remotely initiatives happened. Schools and businesses were closing with only the essential openings and the limited hours. More to come…

"What the hell is essential, Jack? I know it is *essential* that I visit your mother, my smitten-love, Natasha. I shall invent ways to do it, too! Just stay tuned," spouted Joseph.

Later that evening, Jack found Joseph in his studio. He was gazing at his towering art, the wooden sculptures that usually went to the bigger estates and his wealthy clients.

"Hey, Dad, you look like you are contemplating some ideas. Is my work that fabulous?" asked Jack, as he gently poked Dad in a favorite tickle spot.

"You know how proud I am, right?" His twinkling eyes and smile came quickly. But, I have an idea. How do you move these grand wooden sculptures? Use your truck and cranes or what?" he asked, just a bit too inquisitive Jack thought.

"Dad, it is almost midnight. Let's get a good night's rest and I shall show you the videos in the morning, okay?" Jack requested.

"You are right. Night, son. Hey, I know you will like my creative idea."

The next morning arrived. So did Joseph, bright and early to eat a good breakfast.

"I like this. What do you guys call it? Coffee mocha something?" he asked, with his contagious chuckles. "Natasha would love to try today's newest brews!"

"I know you are ready to share your idea, Dad. I bet it includes my truck and cranes? Let's watch that video first," Jack suggested.

"Let's do it!"

The short video was an answer for Joseph. He started to reveal one of his special plans.

"You know how Natasha's window is on the east side, near the parking lot and a side entry? Well, there is a delivery area close by. We could pull up there and rig up something on the crane, so I can visit at Natasha's window," Dad proclaimed, looking like a school boy who won first place in a contest.

"Dad, I know the staff loves you. Loves Natasha. But, they are liable for your safety on the premises. You could not visit the same way or your multiple times, even if they agreed," Jack expressed, as diplomatically as he could. Knowing Joseph, there would be a Plan B, C, D, and whatever.

"Well, I already thought of the no-no retorts and why. So I called the local news channel to see if they would add a feature. Son, the world needs more love now than ever. Natasha and I need to see one another. Smitten for fifty years could be the headliner for a news anchor," continued Joseph, his voice sounding melodic and confident.

Believe it or not, the national news had features on how loved ones could not see parents or a spouse in a nursing home or facility. Later, they showed the creative ways that a few loved ones were visiting, at the windows and assisted with local firemen on their long ladders.

Local anchors adored Joseph's idea, at least for one feature. Meanwhile, Joseph kept quiet with other requests, only for a few days.

"Wow, Dad. You looked awesome on that chair rig near Natasha's window. They showed glimpses of Natasha in her best moments!" touted Janice. Janie was clapping and hugging her Dad at the same time.

"I have some final requests for you kiddos. Get Natasha moved to the bottom floor, the same side, and near a window where I can walk up, see, and talk to her daily. All of you got me the cell phones, so she can hear me as I call from her new window. Our wonderful nurses and caregivers are willing to help," expressed Dad, always with his incredible admiration and pride.

Eventually, his wishes came to fruition. The smitten soul mates—Joseph and Natasha—continued their visits. Inclement weather, Dad's intermittent colds, or the staff shortages meant Dad's less frequent visitations.

There was a beauty in the company of this insidious Alzheimer's disease. Another five years of smitten love between Joseph and Natasha prevailed.

Natasha passed quietly one afternoon. Joseph went to the window to say his loving goodbye. Then the family huddled together with him at the window.

"I'll see you soon, Natasha!" Joseph half-whispered, as he let the tears stream down his cheeks.

The family made a private service in Jack's home studio. There were stunning pictures, selective memorabilia, and the poignant stories. The touching service and a small gathering with catered food became an authentic celebration of Natasha's life.

That evening, Joseph wanted to retire to bed earlier than usual. Loving hugs and kisses. And, such appreciation for their united efforts to celebrate Natasha.

Joseph lay wide awake in bed. "I'll see you soon, Natasha. Still smitten," he half-whispered, letting the tears stream down his cheeks.

The next morning the sunbeams streamed onto his bedside. Jack and his twin sisters went to wake up their Dad. Pausing by the pillow, Jack turned to look. He beckoned to Janice and Janie. They bent over to kiss their Dad's cheeks and hold his hands.

No medical reasons. Joseph slipped away, looking peaceful in the golden sunbeams. Passing during a dreamscape of his still-smitten love for Natasha?

"I believe, with all my heart and soul, that Dad is giving that extra big smooch and hugging Mom. The 'soul mates' to us, better known as the still-smitten lovers. They are now together and so peaceful," Jack affirmed, as he bent over to kiss dear Joseph on his forehead.

"Love you so much, Dad! Love and eternal bliss from all of us."

Pink-raspberry florals for heavenly, serene Natasha,

Affirm and celebrate a family legacy, the smitten lovers,

Floral shapes—intertwining, just like their hearts...

Attentive

Yasmin remembered her technicolor dream. She was attentive when the cleansing winds caressed her and seemed to chant, "I am soulFULL. I am FULL of love." Today, Yasmin was repeating that mantra-chant in the euphoric and golden meadow in front of her log cabin.

The modest log cabin was surrounded by a few cedar trees. Yasmin smelled them vividly in that dream. Then she spotted a Lady Slipper flower, discovered in a cluster of rare slipper-friends. Yasmin found a treasure among the cedars, a path less travelled, even though it was a dream.

Yasmin believed that each dream conveyed whatever she needed. She trusted that her soul rested better in a deep slumber, especially with the fast lane of daily living.

Yasmin affirmed her murmurs about last evening's dreamscape. "I deserve this daily, loving-kind release. This inner space of calm creates a gentle respite and a completion for my soul."

At breakfast, Yasmin sipped her green tea and munched slowly on a scone. As she peeled back the layers of her juicy orange, something else resonated. Last month's affective treasures and the lifetime lessons were dynamic. Yasmin was grateful for the online summits with such rallying, poignant, and novel messages.

A recent healing summit and those vibrant messages kept Yasmin compelled to write. A valued legacy for herself was penned in today's journal entry. These written acknowledgments and the innate honor nestled close to her heart.

She took a minute to reread her written acknowledgments. Yasmin appreciated and felt her peace of mind, a tranquil solitude.

I feel divine and worthy. I love myself completely. It is an unconditional love in the company of a genuine forgiveness.

Is the half-empty glass missing a sustenance?

Is the half-full glass brimming with an abundance?

Yasmin made her attentive and soul-filled choices...

GO
live
YOUR
life

Mountain ranges of New Mexico beckon with the Aspen summons,

DJ and Irving decided to explore and live life to the max,

Unforeseen white-out squalls, the berserk-blizzard winds, and a life force began to alter that master plan...

Aspen Summons

"Is this our vacation rental? Any log cabins? Can you see in this wild, white-out blizzard? Think anyone is here for a key? Wait, I see…" DJ was rambling, with all of the non-stop questions.

"Whoa, is that a light? Head this way. NO, THIS WAY!" Irving hollered and pointed, especially when he spotted another flicker.

"What light? I do not… Okay dude, here we go. Hey, this truck is not acting like four-wheel drive," DJ shouted, as the dicey blizzard was kicking in fast and furiously.

"Get as close as you can. I gotta try! Whatever is by that light," Irving bellowed, wrestling to open his door.

DJ squinted hard, catching a glimpse of him. Was Irving actually headed toward a log cabin?

The mountain ranges of New Mexico beckoned again. He brought Irving to this timeshare with the fall summons of Aspen beauty. This trip, DJ had coaxed his cousin to try the early winter allure.

Berserk. No blizzard was predicted or anticipated. Way too early for these kind of white-out squalls. Actually, it was a record-biting and icy jolt for this part of New Mexico.

His desolate daydreams were cut short, as Irving was straining to reopen his passenger door. DJ leaned over, tugged, and yanked the handle.

Irving disappeared in a white-out gust. In a few seconds, Irving reappeared, totally snow-crusted and swearing.

"Damn it! Damn, this door and handle! They were like icebound Siberia. Gotta key, dude! Guy warned this baby, our wild blizzard, was going to be horrendous. Hoped that we got the fire to last and this key would open our arctic cabin. I dunno, buddy!" fretted Irving, with an exasperated, anxious stare and the latest updates.

"So sorry, man! Where do ya think I should drive? Need all the f***** help to track down cabin seven. Pray for a miracle, RIGHT NOW!" shouted DJ, as a sudden lessening of the flare-up gales and the white-outs gave a few bursts of clarity.

"How come we can see? Buddy, I did ask for a miracle. C'mon Archangel Michael, we need your protection and HELP! RIGHT NOW!" Irving hollered, raising his arms up to the ceiling dome of DJ's truck.

"Dude, look that way—log cabins, the A-frames. Here we go! Hang tough, my mystical genius of a cousin," asserted DJ, laughing heartily from his beer belly.

They found number seven, crashing out of the truck doors. DJ and Irving tried to rush in the ramped-up snow drifts, hoping their key was a winner, more than any lotto tickets they had bought.

Perhaps, an Irving miracle was in the works? Never mind, just grab, stumble, fall down, and drag their stuff. Do it before Mother Nature's intention for a few saintly, celestial moments and their suck-it-up momentum was a goner.

Indoors! DJ and Irving were giving the high five slaps, but only for a few seconds. Their panic-stricken eyes haunted one another. They needed to start the fire.

The wood stove had a long pipe, extending from its backside to the adjacent wall and toward the A-frame roof. One, two, three, and suddenly, the fourth undertaking was the charmer and a definite adrenalin rush.

"I need a beer!" broadcasted DJ, searching through the tossed piles of gear for any sign of a cooler. "Lost, but found!"

"Wha la, my cousin. To our heroic efforts and the supernatural from somewhere, maybe more archangels like Jophiel and Ariel or their angelic troops!" bragged Irving, revealing a colossal smile plastered on his face, one that DJ had never seen.

Their gala spree and a boastful spirit started too early. This possessed, unhinged storm and the menacing, imposing gusts blew the snow through the minuscule door cracks. The wood stove flames dwindled and snuffed out at the higher elevation. Of course—no service on their cell phones.

Not exactly an envied vacation with a restful slumberland. There were two days and two nights of the panic moments, an ever-present angst, and the imagined horrors of being trapped.

No partying and the cousin-banter like this fall. Irving and DJ were grabbing their sandwiches with a coke for all meals. Caffeine boosts were necessary, really urgent by the second day and night of their wigged-out sleep.

"Who is getting up to watchdog the fire tonight?" mumbled Irving, sounding and looking zonked.

No answer, as DJ was already snoring. Irving crashed in a few seconds. Both of them woke up, shivering and cussing. DJ stumbled to the entry, in spite of the ruckus, yanked the door, and pivoted quickly. Irving was already in his ecstatic face.

"Look. Damn, LOOK! The early sun, no blizzard, and a stunning blue sky. Hey man, check out the drifts at our entry and over the windows!" yelled DJ, even though Irving was already shaking his shoulders.

"Free at last! Torment, begone! We can dig a smaller trail at our front entry and onto the deck. No worries, buddy, especially compared to the last two days and those eves!"

proclaimed Irving, starting his uncontrollable laughs. He made DJ crack up during their dig-outta-everywhere mania.

They had only two brooms and a couple of lids from the kitchen pots, but they finished their adrenalin-rush gig. No doubt, the altitude contributed to their delirious attitude.

"In a flash, we dig. Heave-ho, heave-ho. Chop-chop, Irving and DJ dig like lunatics. I need another sandwich. This time, I am having a cold blast of beer!" replied DJ, in a wicked low and spooky voice. Then he toddled along the small pathway like an abdominal snowman.

Both dudes took a restful break, dragging out a cooler for their seat. The sandwiches and beer tasted much better on day four. "Vacation heaven for the rest of the week" or so claimed the forecast guy in the office cabin.

Irving and DJ decided right away. Off on a snowmobile adventure and the winding trails to the top of Evergreen Mountain. They were happy campers.

"You are the Dallas dudes with a bravado to dig it—our vista at the 11,000 foot elevation!" confirmed Ron.

Today's snowmobile venture was the early afternoon excursion. Off the mountain top before dusk was Ron's promise, so that Mama Nature's critters would not enjoy all the dudes—as a feast of famine.

"Hey, dudes! Your snowmobile gear. Are you ready for this lovable, hippy guy who ended up in New Mexico about fifteen years ago? Fly fishing come spring and summer. Snowmobile dare devil in the winter. That is me, Big D city-slickers," Ron drawled, as he flung a super-long, stocking hat to the left side of his dreadlocks.

Evergreen Mountain and the vista were breathtaking and refreshing on that cold, sunny afternoon. All of them raced around a vista-top meadowland with the coyote-like howls and an intermittent, flying arm, much like the rodeo days of Irving and DJ.

Ron was a crazed dude, his dreadlocks and a stocking hat whipping in the winds. Photos pleazzee—beside the posted elevation in hooded outfits, super face masks, and the ski goggles to boot. Of course, Ron was photobombing every one of their selfies.

"Hey, what's happening to the weather, Ron?" hollered DJ, feeling a faster heartbeat underneath the wintry garb. He turned, only to catch the wacky sight. Ron was already off on a crazed runabout, hollering something.

"DJ, that is another front! Headed *here* way faster than a nightmare. When did that happen? We just had sunshine and took photos! We gotta get the heck off this mountain top, NOW!" shouted Irving.

Both of them waved their exhausted arms to Ron dude. Finally, crazed Ron headed toward them at top speed.

"Dudes, we gotta go—now!" Ron bellowed, blasting off as DJ and Irving bolted to their snowmobiles.

Racing down the narrow, steep trails. Not dusk, but an ominous sky and this fast-moving front gave way to the mounting fears. Would they be able to beat the monstrous squalls, zigzagging down the narrowest trails?

A sleet-snow mix ramped up. The tormenting winds became relentless, making it almost impossible to see much of anything through their ski goggles.

"Archangels, ascended masters, and guardian angels, I am calling upon you to protect and guide us," murmured Irving, chanting under his ski mask and the hooded snowsuit.

DJ and Ron made it to the base of the mountain. Fifteen minutes or longer? They had almost crashed, skidding to a stop near a door for the rental excursions.

Watching and squinting. Listening for Irving's snowmobile. They had to take turns going inside, but never said a word. DJ had been blown against the door, when he sensed that Irving might be trudging towards him.

"I am coming. I got your back, buddy!" DJ screamed, to no avail with another burst of white-out squalls and the whipping winds. He smashed right into his cousin.

Locked together, their arms and bodies intertwined, somehow DJ and Irving crashed into the door. Both of them got dragged indoors with Ron's hollers and help.

An evening deja vu, this time with three dudes. Irving told them about his close call, a tree-lined trail, and ditching his snowmobile. Irving shared his chanting, what he did all the way down the mountain trails.

"Dallas dude, you are connected to a lovable, hippy guy. Judgements about any chanting or the archangels? Hey, the angelic forces or something made sure. I did not lose my hippy, stocking hat," Ron half-whispered, as if the guardian spirits were present. All of them cracked up, as Ron flipped his long stocking hat over the front of his face and 'round and 'round his dreadlocks.

Blue skies with a nostalgic sunshine, the wavy snow drifts, and their last high five's arrived the next morning. Was it Mother Earth and her pure vibrational energy?

Back at cabin seven, there was a note duct-taped on the cupboard. It was scrawled by the office guy. "Another FRONT. You guys can beat it, but head home SOON. Drop the key in office box. GOOD LUCK!"

Deja vu for the Dallas dudes—racing and throwing gear wherever it landed in the truck. No interstates for hours, just the winding roads and this huge mountain range of New Mexico.

"Wassup, DJ? That front is haunting us the entire way. We are barely ahead of this white-out blizzard. What the heck? What kinda BAD karma is chasing us now?" added Irving, in a voice no longer able to mask a wicked nervous tone.

"Hey, cousin, you brought on the miracles. Start that Evergreen Mountain chanting. Irving buddy, leave out that last negative vibe and go for the GOOD karma," bellowed DJ, as he sped along the isolated roadways.

Out yonder in the wild, Dallas dudes racing against the next front,

Forever-winding roads and a racing truck—against nature's clock,

Strong-willed calls for celestial guidance and only the good vibes...

Cosmic Vibrations

The ophthalmologist was recommended by a colleague, Artemus, in the fine arts college. Eliza intended to ask him if the doctor was local or in another town.

She sent out a positive vibe with her thoughts. *An outstanding choice! My intention is to greet Artemus. I foreshadow that our meet up is today.*

Coming out of a practice room with her alto sax, Eliza smiled. There was Artemus at the elevator.

"How did your practice go today? Ready for your performance evaluation with the gifted ones in our music department?" he teased. Artemus made quotation marks, high in the air, as he spoke of the gifted ones.

"Sure! Bring on the gifted faculty to judge, if I am a treasure and quite worthy of my promotion and precious tenure," declared the feisty and fun-loving Eliza, mimicking his quotation marks with her long index fingers.

Both of them cracked up. A gifted colleague bolted past them a few minutes later. Unbelievable! They paused and continued chuckling, making hysterical faces, as they went down to the first floor on the elevator.

"Oh, I met to ask you about that eye doc that you recommended last week. Is he local or in another town?" queried Eliza, as they exited from the front foyer.

"Local. I got his contact in my phone. Here it is—Dr. K. Kowalczyk, but he is cool with Dr. K. The Polish have a lot of consonants, only a few vowels. He has a super reputation, plus his eye surgeries are sought after by numerous people in the Southwest," proclaimed Artemus.

"Hey, thanks! I shall talk with you, after you know what!"

The next week was her perfecto-performance time and a fast appointment with Dr. Kowalczyk due to a cancellation. Dr. K. was in the morning. By early afternoon, Eliza would have to wow the gifted faculty. Her thoughts turned to the munchies.

I am starving. Seafood, a veggie medley, and the harvest rice sounds yummy. A toast of vino to add to the zest and my bon appetite. Next week? I am ready, actually quite psyched.

Next week in Dr. Kowalczyk's office, his wife gave a friendly welcome as Eliza filled out the paperwork. His wife helped with scheduling surgeries and business details, so she came from the front office. There was a knock at Eliza's patient door.

"Hi there, I am Dr. Kowalczyk. Everyone calls me Dr. K. and that is superlative. Have any Polish friends? And, I surmise, you are able to *spell* their last names." Dr. K. teased, with a quirky laugh.

"Hey, my mother is part Polish and Austrian. Kielbasa and pierogi are still a treat!" Eliza bragged, already liking his demeanor.

Dr. K's exam was high tech, intriguing, and explained well with each procedure. Right away, Eliza commended his teaching style. He was quick to remark.

"In the presence of renowned professors, I kick up things a notch!"

Eliza laughed heartily and agreed with a quick thumbs-up sign. Next on Dr. K's agenda was whether she wanted exotic, tinted, or the clear contacts.

Well, that inquiry started everything. Samples of the new rage like cat's eyes and the new tints with exotic names were presented. Lastly, the clear contacts were mentioned, like an afterthought offering.

Eliza was handed an exotic mermaid mirror, whenever she tried each sample. Uproarious laughter with all—Dr. K., his wife, and the staff—as Eliza posed theatrically with each pair. Then something caught Eliza off guard.

Her trendy outfit and trying the matching or the mismatched contacts? Is Dr. K. touching my hand or my arm gently during all of the hysteria or is that just his demeanor? Perhaps, it is my imagination.

Next year's annual exam was scheduled, unless she needed an appointment for other eye concerns. Eliza was off and racing to her early afternoon performance with the gifted earthlings. She was psyched and thinking confidently during her drive.

ALL is ready to happen—my promotion and precious tenure. Butterflies in my tummy are an earthly thing, because I am psyched and nervous-happy. Wait, take my deeper breaths for a peace and calm, before I park, stroll, and enter my envisioned golden door confidently.

Artemus was waiting outdoors, down a walkway near a redbud tree. Eliza sprang out the front door, starting her jive-dancing down the granite steps.

"I guess that means that you pulled off the mesmerizing moments with the gifted ones, Eliza? A magnifico performance?" Artemus queried, standing at the walkway to her right.

"Artemus, what a wondrous surprise. Yes! Ohh, yes! My alto sax shindig is a done deal. Indeed, a perfecto performance," she touted. Then Eliza went straight toward him, jiving along the entire walkway, flinging her slender arms and long legs.

They hugged like a pair of exuberant kiddos. They grinned and cracked up, the authentic amusement emanating from two elated hearts.

"Calls for a celebration, my loco Eliza. My treat at the Dips and Scoops Creamery? I know that you luv-v-v ice cream, but you better get a whopping sundae or a banana split!"

"Artemus, thank you! I shall have a grande sundae, if you please!" Eliza asserted, smacking her lips and rubbing her tummy.

They hugged like two bears again. Off to chill out and celebrate the feisty and deserving fire in Eliza's belly. Suddenly, Eliza stopped in her footprints.

"Hey, Artemus, you already have tenure and had to perform. A lot of those gifted faculty must have judged you as well?" she asked, looking quizzically. He never gave her a sneak preview, just his gifted-ones whimsy.

"Hey, we practice our alto saxes in the practice rooms. We have attended our performances, not just for tenure and the promotions. My jiving and loco Eliza, you got a style and an obvious talent. I was not worried—about you or myself a few years ago," Artemus confided, displaying a transparent confidence.

On that note, another big-bear hug could not be missed. They scampered for that whopping, sweet refreshment at the Dips and Scoops Creamery. Today became a day of splendor for Eliza's journal of affirmations.

Life in academe progressed with the tidbits of drama, the lofty fun, academic politics, and the teaching-performing passion for both of them. Earlier promotion to "full profs" entered the loop. Eliza and her super plan came to fruition.

Eliza gifted Artemus with a classic alto sax, a fine eatery, and the super festive delights. Bon appetit and the cheerio-vino toasts topped the "full prof" celebration.

There was a Bermuda weekend cruise, when Eliza's "full prof" arrived on the campus scene. The dynamic duo and the best of friends became the lively castaways for her celebration.

In the meantime, Eliza tried out a nearby church that was non-denominational. They had a metaphysical bookstore, interesting classes, precious yoga, a labyrinth walk, and the intimate drumming circles as well. She attended the evening meditation group as much as possible.

Dr. K. started attending the same church. After the late Sunday service, Eliza often stayed for coffee. Last week, Dr. K. waved and came to visit, only as most folks were departing. Eliza began to wonder.

No mystery or surprise? All my fortuitous stories happen in the faculty parking lot and now, the church parking lot.

"Eliza, I am losing my vision to an eye disease that is progressive. I shall be able to see with special glasses, but no more eye surgeries. My marriage ended in a dicey divorce. I cannot envision my life ahead," Dr. K. confided.

"I am so sorry! I had annual eye appointments, never knew all of this was happening," she replied, almost in a whisper.

"Eliza, my marriage has been a rocky terrain with peaks and darker valleys. No children, thank goodness, given our dicey divorce. But, I got to be honest. That day in the office when I met you? I lusted about you. Nowadays, I am beyond distress with my failing eye sight and a limited future without performing eye surgeries," Dr. K. confessed, his voice starting to tremble.

"I wish that I could respond perfectly, but I am...well, I am empathic, shocked, and a little unsettled—all at once," responded Eliza.

"Oh, I am not going to hit on you, Eliza. This is my first time to share anything with anyone. You are a free spirit, attentive, and empathic. I saw that on your appointments across the years," Dr. K. offered, looking at Eliza with his troubled eyes.

Eliza and Dr. K. were the last to leave the parking lot. Something shifted in her core being. Eliza talked and empathized. But, no hugs for Dr. K. Just kindness and a gentle touch on his arm when they departed.

Perhaps, it was his vulnerability or the way Dr. K. looked when he talked to her. Eliza just knew—when things shifted in her being and to honor that moment.

Church services and her spiritual practices moved forward. Eliza felt Dr. K's disconnection and his vibrational energy. No more over-talking about his repetitive stories of distress.

He was not trying the releases from the spiritual classes. Dr. K. began something else. He introduced his repetitive talk again—with two women, particularly after the evening meditation classes.

Meanwhile, the academic journeys and living a spirit-filled life ensued. Artemus and Eliza were entrusted friends. They supported students with performances at different university events. They became gifted mentors to the green professors, including their tenure-track and any of the promotion peaks and valleys.

Politics changed with the new chairs or deans, but the notorious environments were reinforced at the national conferences or the recent workshops. Horrific politics, sexual harassment issues, the ramped-up power plays in departments, and no mentors for a promotion or tenure were a norm for the faculty at diverse universities. Yesterday's return from New York was a ditto of those distressing sagas.

"Can you imagine their daily challenges?" implored Eliza.

"Only imagine in my mindful heart. Yet, it strikes a chord that we decided to choose our campus. I call you loco and feisty Eliza, but you have never been penalized, ostracized, or not given a personal space to be a free spirit," Artemus replied, always in his slow and gentle tone, looking deeper into Eliza's eyes.

"So true! Right now. Wanna pause and go for a favorite walk? Our college woods on the campus, a conservation land of peace and solace. You wanna?" Eliza inquired, looking deeper into his eyes, not ignoring a definite shift in her core being.

"Let's do it!"

The springtime beauty, the whispering pines, and a compelling trek into the campus woods offered a tranquility and a transformative spirit. Sunbeams came through the forested pines in their favorite spot. Both of their meditative breaths—deeper and soothing—came naturally.

"Artemus, my entrusted friend, I am so grateful for our paths crossing. I believe unexpected paths and events are no coincidence," Eliza intoned gently, her mystical gaze returning to his twinkling eyes.

"Listen, my loco and feisty Eliza. You are a cherished friend on this earthly planet and way out there," Artemus gestured upward and whispered, as they embraced with the big-bear hugs.

Today, the old barn's window panes in Artemus and Eliza's beloved campus woods revealed one flower of innate beauty,

Musical duos, the dialogues, and their friendship remained an effortless joy on this springtime day of radiant sunbeams,

Their feisty and loco play was destined to foster an unconditional caring and a deepening friendship...

The Veil of Night Enchantment

Gently floating upon the water, Lulu listened to an enchanting melody that played within the lake ripples. Lake ripples caressed her stretching legs and arms. Lulu was free-floating with the beginning dusk and an evening of enchantment. Sublime pleasures.

As the darker veil of night began to envelope Lulu, a magical moonbeam spotlighted a long pathway upon the lake ripples. The mystical moonbeam caressed each of the mesmerizing ripples. Sublime pleasures.

Lulu waded slowly towards the rock steps, letting the lake ripples continue to envelope her slim, svelte legs. She glanced upward, tossing a kiss to the glowing moonbeam that lead toward her lake bungalow. Sublime pleasures.

Later that evening, a trance-like solace emerged as Lulu closed her eyes. Lulu breathed deeply, closer to the midnight realm.

The veil of night enchantment had arrived. The loons were echoing, as Lulu drifted off into her stunning and infinite dreamscapes.

AFTER DARK

The secret to
happiness is
freedom... And
the secret to
freedom is
courage

Destiny and Jeff found a beauty and the illusive beast,

Searching, exploring, and the distress of separation,

Their freedom and happiness to be discovered...

Beauty or The Beast

Destiny and Jeff met at a bi-monthly meeting. Jeff worked for the town, a relatively new civil engineer. The townies often got the "first dibs" on any job openings. The right political vibe and the family connections mattered.

Jeff loved his outdoor projects, not so much the political scenarios in this close-knit town. Destiny attended a few meetings of interest. When Jeff gave a final report on his civil engineering project, she gazed up from her comical doodling towards the podium.

He was a cute guy, a different personality from the usual town presenters. The town agenda was concluded, after his intriguing and a thought-provoking presentation.

Destiny took a longer time, filling her funky backpack, until he returned to the front row. She decided to congratulate Jeff for his execution and the triumph, as this project had been placed on the back burner for at least a year.

"Hi there, Jeff. My name is Destiny. Lived here long enough to realize that your project was not exactly a top priority. My compliments and the kudos for your accomplishment!" she offered, with a stunning smile, walking confidently towards Jeff's seat for a handshake.

"Thanks! Did not get the thumbs-up sign for two years. I was a new kid on the block, a bit suspect," Jeff offered, sharing a smirk and his self-assured handshake.

"Well, my intentional hope is that you fast forward the relevant town projects, keeping the dream troopers in the loop. Really looking forward to the next meeting," Destiny added, strolling away with a confident stride and a dazzling smile, affirming her engaging and upbeat attitude.

Fall, winter, and spring flew by, as she chose to attend a majority of the town meetings. Destiny was sketching for the local galleries and an adjunct professor of English at a nearby private college.

Five interviews for full-time positions with tenure-track and super benefits remained her beacons of light. Jeff and Destiny had been dating, pursuing a transparent caring and a unique rapport. They were somewhat surprised by their own welcoming, whimsical, and unconventional families.

New York, Minnesota, Massachusetts, California, and Colorado were prime reasons for a ruckus celebration. Jeff and Destiny conjured up the enterprising festivities for each family and their best friends. Destiny was not sure about a final decision, but really liked two collegiate offers and the intrinsic appeals.

"Destiny, you are impressive with five out of five offers! Naturally, I have given the thumbs-up sign to your clever, ingenious writings. Guess I am not biased, huh?" teased Jeff, drawing Destiny closer with a wink, his awesome embrace, and the magnificent kisses.

"Ah, ever so sublime, our elevated kisses. Truthfully, I cannot make up my mind and heart about my two choices. Here in Massachusetts, which is closer to our families and you. Or the new beginnings in Boulder, Colorado that offer a top notch department and the talented colleagues," Destiny began to share, as the romantic interlude gave way to their valued dialogues.

"It comes down to an authentic passion, the yearning, and your conscious choice. I have been to Colorado with my college friends. Boulder is damn gorgeous, an eclectic region. You can guess which job offer that I want you to muse, ponder, and contemplate. I shall never hide my desire and wishful partying for the Massachusetts destiny, irresistible Destiny!" Jeff confessed, grinning with his purposeful pun.

In the late summer, Destiny departed for Boulder in her pick-up with the seasonal clothes, limited kitchenware, and the sentimental treasures, since a furnished apartment was a done deal. Jeff was an eager traveler across the fabulous USA, respecting and admiring her verve, professional brilliance heightened with a savvy intuition, and her judgements.

"Let's make our journey a tour de force, an adventure the entire way, Jeff. You are staying for a few weeks, so we can explore the Boulder scene and scope out everything! I truly want you to visit. I shall return regularly," promised Destiny, wondering if she committed to Boulder, if there would be equally good reasons and a splendid karma for Jeff's relocation.

Both of them accepted the academic politics. By the third year, Destiny would need to decide. Stay or change universities. Perfect timing to receive meaningful recommendations from an assistant professor journey, her teaching and research, and the student evaluations. Plus, it was a "realistic norm" for a tenure-track and the promotion pursuits at any new university.

"I am coming home after December finals, staying until mid-January when our spring semester begins. Jeff, I adore the diversity here, but I am thrilled to fly home, too!" Destiny revealed, as they conversed on FaceTime and pantomimed the kisses. A few years, the mutual visits, and the special renewals happened with their dynamite, almost surreal flashbacks.

"I am getting you at the airport and want you to stay at my digs. How do ya feel about that intent and my suggestion? We can bombard our families and best friends, whenever they miss us too much. My cozy condo gives us private time and our space, just like our cross-country visits. Is that a feel-good vibe for you…for us?" Jeff inquired, looking elated and sporting his awesome grins displayed on her phone.

"Definitely! Our visits and the exquisite moments in Boulder have been at my comfy apartment. Love all of it, Jeff!" Destiny whispered, in her lowest, sexy voice. She watched, until the caring images ended. Jeff had signed off with a bunch of winks and his virtual hugs.

Super flight, no delays. Stupendous holidays. There were plenty of stellar moments for them, plus the bombarding scenarios with each family and the endearing friends. The captivating weeks dropped out of sight.

Return to the airport and soar back to Boulder. It was not long. Destiny started the spring semester in mid-January, the same month that she received an unexpected call.

"Destiny, this is Dr. Stonegate in Massachusetts. How are you doing out there in lovely Boulder?" he inquired.

"Oh, Dr. Stonegate! Well, what a surprise. My faculty and students are a joy and quite spunky. You have traveled to Boulder, so you know the enticing appeals. Might I inquire why you called me?" Destiny asked very slowly, trying to be diplomatic and imagine the ultimate reason for this weekend call.

"Well, you were an esteemed finalist for our position! The second-choice candidate has not worked. Plain and simple. I am calling to request your reconsideration of our offer. Your present tenure-track years would apply, plus a salary with a notable increase. Your national acclaim at conferences is terrific, especially in such a short timespan. Destiny, no answer is warranted right now, but please…give us very serious consideration. I could fly you here for our required interview in a month, if you agree?" Dr. Stonegate asked, revealing his kind-hearted and respectful regard.

"My word, I am honored. Taken off-guard, as you might suspect. I could visit my family during a small break with a weekend reprieve. Dr. Stonegate, I want to solidify that this interview is kept confidential. You understand my request, I am sure," added Destiny, in a self-assured voice.

"Of course! Our intent is not to jeopardize your future. Honestly, we want you as our tenured faculty. I suspect that your colleagues and administrators are well aware of Destiny's reputation at conferences and any additional offers that are happening. Our faculty dialogue regularly about better programs and certain individuals to pursue. You are perceptive and can surmise the professional grapevine about Destiny's talents and your lively personality," Dr. Stonegate added, again with his gentle manner and a few chuckles.

"Why, thank you for those compliments and such candor. I look forward to this semester and want to keep in touch with your updates. Really appreciate that you called my cell phone during the weekend, Dr. Stonegate," Destiny stated confidently, knowing that he understood her message.

Once they hung up, Destiny listened to jazz music and danced wildly around her apartment. Time would tell. She drifted off to sleep, dreaming of a serene beach, its Caribbean waters, and her luxurious swim. A bronzed guy came to the beach, diving underwater and swam her way. Swimming closer, there was something so familiar, but Destiny woke up. Foggy thoughts took over.

Alarm clock. No, my cell phone is ringing. Is it already the morning? Okay, Destiny-diva.... when and where did I toss my phone? Probably while dancing so blithely and before my serene and unfinished dreamscape. Hey...I need to listen to my voicemail, whenever there is a message. Where the heck did I pitch my phone during my exotic and rollicking dance spree?

"Hey, Jeff. I am leaving another voicemail. Yep, we are playing phone tag today. Off to teach a terrific class and head to two faculty meetings. This evening is better for our wondrous call. Make it a magnificent and entertaining day!" she added, envisioning Jeff's fun expressions.

They talked that eve. Destiny updated Jeff about her unexpected call and the offer. Time would tell with an interview in another month. Both of them were optimistic about the interview and another together-time in Massachusetts.

In the next month, Destiny completed the required portfolio for this year's evaluation with her chairperson and a peer-review committee. Flying colors with the peer encouragements happened. Destiny's elation was tempered only by that surprise call, the collegiate offer in Massachusetts and her interview in a few days.

"I have to head right back to Boulder, as you know. What an amazing interview, Jeff. I have to decide in a few months, as they want to do an earlier contract. Are you still debating about your job here? Did Boulder come through with an offer?" queried Destiny, noticing his immediate smile.

"Destiny, I got a nice phone call before you came for this interview. The Boulder job is mine. I did not want to overshadow your interview, until both of us knew how the faculty and those administrative meet-ups evolved. Now, we know! Togetherness or our visits?" Jeff asked gently, looking softly into Destiny's eyes.

"You have an incredible look right now, Jeff. I hear everything. I want to talk about us and our offers, right?" Destiny offered, reaching for his hands and sensing a stirring of profound and joyous feelings.

"My caring is beyond phenomenal. We evolved as the best of friends and the special lovers. Perhaps, we are a bit fearful or anxious about making the wrong or impulsive career moves. One precious gift—without a doubt? I am not fearful about us, Destiny," he confirmed, drawing Destiny closer and holding tight.

"Jeff, I know that our togetherness is an ultimate friendship and a unique love. My intuitive belly or gut feels our apprehension about career pathways and the different locales. Endearing families and friends in Massachusetts, yet significant friends for us in our eclectic and beautiful Boulder," Destiny reaffirmed, holding tighter with their kisses.

They rocked gently in a longer embrace, a solace that rejuvenated an amazing synchrony. Both of them fell fast asleep, intertwined and dreaming in technicolor.

The next morning, Jeff's phone was ringing on the kitchen counter. His boss was relaying something about a new project. When Jeff hung up, he stared at enchanting Destiny, sitting like a yoga queen on the couch.

"The moment my boss talked, I felt a shift in my gut. No kidding, my blissful spirit. I listened to the new project, but felt a beastly critter roaming wildly in my gut. The same beastly critter with most of my projects. This time? No resonance or any desire to tackle this new project. Obvious cliques with old town politics, my relentless hurdles, and a projected two or three years with this new project. Time to move forward, Destiny." Jeff stared at her for a few seconds.

Beauty or the beastly critter returning to my gut," Jeff repeated, twice with a striking confidence, a faraway gaze, and his head nods. Then came his emerging and engaging grin.

"Today, you definitely knew, didn't you? Jeff, an unexpected moment arrived for us! So amazing," Destiny murmured, in a softer and coaxing voice, as Jeff walked purposefully towards the couch.

"There is such thing as destiny, Jeff," she whispered.

"My belief for a long time. And now? I really entrust this timing and our gift," Jeff replied tenderly, sitting down on the couch to kiss Destiny.

It was a bestowal, these moments of knowing. Their gifts without a price tag finally arrived.

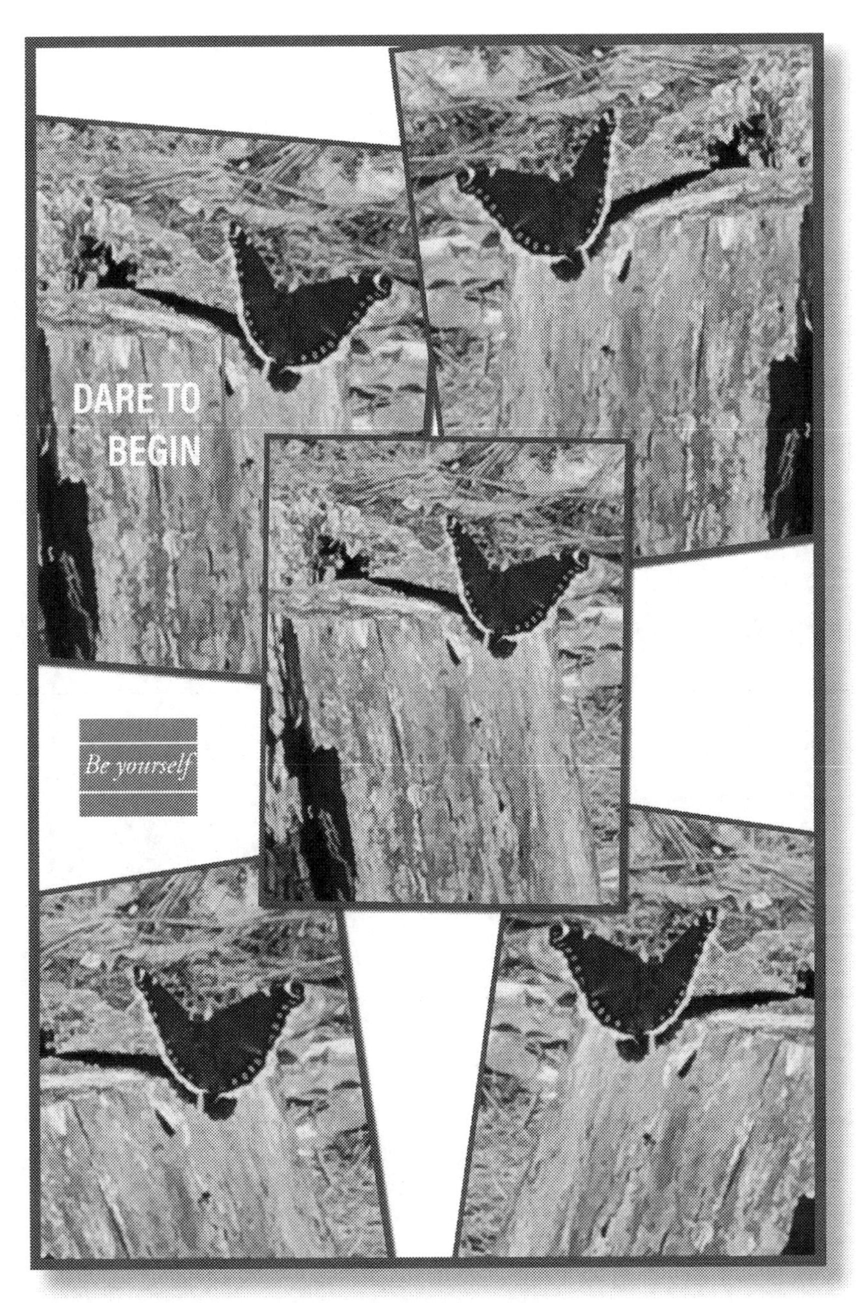

Daring to confront beauty or the beast,

Travels are surrendered to their bestowal,

Arrival of Destiny and Jeff's gifts without a price tag...

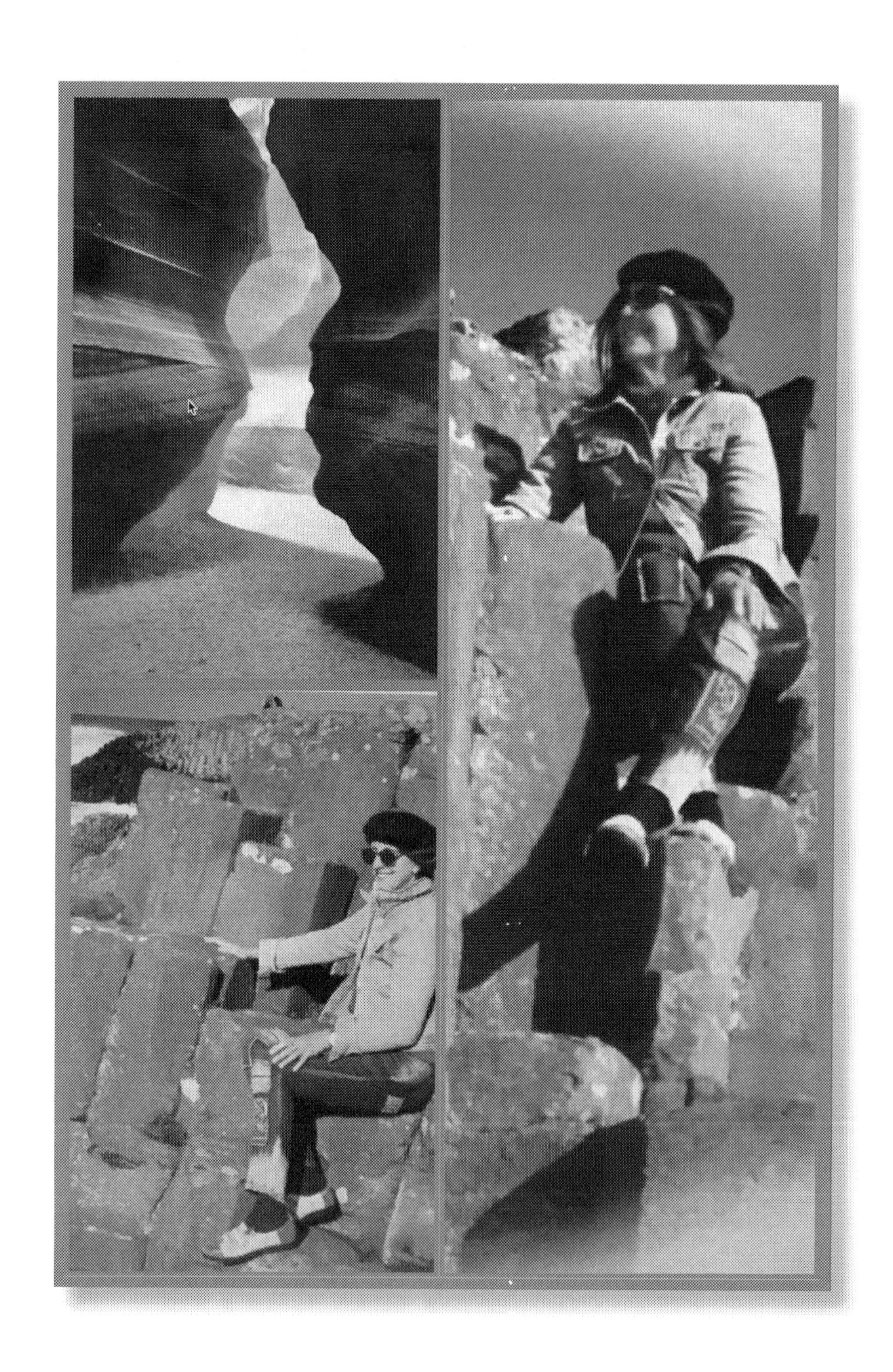

Pursuits of the opportune travels,

Doors closing, but new doors opening,

Healing pinnacles became Vickie's serendipity...

Healing Pinnacles

"No way, Vickie, I cannot attend this year. Just do it! The opportune timing for you, especially after the advocacy and a loving-kind caregiving for your beloved and elderly parents," urged Arlene.

"Truths be known—my welcome recharge and a tithe from my parents, the guardian angels. Here I come, Dominican Republic. It is only a half hour to Punta Cana from the airport. All the events and workshops are on-site at the resort. Plus, the culinary delights, ultramarine waters, and the holistic venues with the acclaimed presenters," expounded Vickie.

"I promise that next year will be my reprieve. I am already *envisioning* for both of us. Takes place in Sedona, a paramount healing mecca!" relayed Arlene, reaffirming her usual eagerness.

"Yes, Sedona will be our special haven. Dah, dah! I have a timeshare that I can exchange, hopefully for the exact site of the events in Punta Cana. Or a sister-resort that works splendidly. Wow, a get-away for an entire week, not just the two-day workshop experiences and those milestones!" proclaimed Vickie, prancing and twirling around Arlene's homestead. Arlene's five cats enjoyed the prancing, but they boot-scooted quickly with Vickie's exotic and ultra-jive maneuvers.

The vacation exchange with an agent worked out fine, almost effortlessly. The direct flights matched well with her workplace, a vacation time, and the events. The pre-registration process was a walk in the park. As a matter of fact, Vickie went for a stroll in a favorite park, appreciating this endorphin-high and her inspirational talks with Arlene.

Next week could not arrive fast enough. Finally, she was at the gate and boarding. Vickie was ready to be jetting to fabulous Punta Cana.

"Thanks so much. I love a vista and the fabulous clouds. Appreciate the smiles as you jostle around, until I nestle at my window seat," Vickie jested, with her athletic maneuvers to sit down her bootie, minus the usual fanfare.

"No worries and our pleasure. My hubby and I were speculating about who likes the window seats? Now, we have met a joyful person who adores a vista and the amazing clouds," Amelia offered, revealing a genuine amusement.

"I can high hurdle over the two seats, when I catapult to the restroom. A direct and shorter flight, so I doubt that either of you will witness that spectacular feat," quipped Vickie.

Their mutual banter was evident throughout the flight. Turned out that they were vacationing at the same resort in Punta Cana. Disembark, do the passport procedures, and use a transfer for a resort van. All happened with the minimal lines. Their mutual rapport was a foreshadowing of the next splendor.

"The event starts this mid-week and your rental is for the entire week, right?" repeated Amelia and Elton, almost in concert. They laughed, admitting how often they were on a similar wavelength.

"Well, now—both of you divulged the low down, almost simultaneously!" acknowledged Vickie. She was rather infatuated with this fun-filled couple.

"We are crashing in our room, but want to check out the main dining in an hour or so for the all-inclusive meals. Are you free and do you dare to join us?" inquired Elton, with a mischievous look, which triggered their next laughing binge.

"Let's do it! Elton and Amelia, I am game. A daring diva, I am!" Vickie spouted, in a heartbeat. A nice valet in a golf cart interrupted their charismatic moments.

Vickie settled quickly. Funky and lighter tops, the casual shorts, stunning bathing suits, and the no-iron, comfy outfits for different entertainers or the event gatherings. Then relaxing for a spell on a heavenly bed right near her impressive balcony with a breathtaking view. Then vamoose—for a coffee at the charming lobby next to the main dining room.

Like minds and hearts think alike? Amelia, Elton, and Vickie were on a search-and-find mission for the exotic coffee machines. They bumped into one another near the chic espresso cups and cappuccino mugs.

"Whoa, looks like all of us dig our next mission with a rather slick timing," bragged Vickie, tossing her long auburn hair. She paused to strike a comical pose.

"Vickie, you are a hoot! Our mission is accomplished. Everyone was bragging about a lavish lobby and the exceptional coffee machines on our flight. We beat the tamer gang," verified Amelia, as she beamed and gestured towards a quaint cafe table with the azure-tile motif.

"Let's sit at one of those exquisite cafe tables and cushy chairs,"offered Elton, stopping to take along a plate of delectable fruits and small snacks. Vickie was quick to detect that Elton never saw Amelia's animated gestures, but he picked out the identical table in the cafe. Same wave length, again.

A weekend forecast showed the ravishing days, chock full of their Dominican-alluring sunshine. Ideal conditions for swimming in the teal ocean waters, daily kayaking, and the ultimate parasailing. Vickie was peppy and full of pranks when the outdoor activities were available.

Neat acquaintances happened whenever Vickie ventured to explore and partake of a playtime. Oh, quite the beau for her parasail partner. They were carefree spirits, enjoying a few swims and a beach visit after the panoramic beauty of parasailing.

Vickie made plans to meet Amelia and Elton at the Italian and seafood eateries offered throughout the resort. They sat together during the grandeur of the evening entertainment, if their bionic eyes spotted one another in the majestic theaters.

Their instant connections prompted the phone and address exchanges, long before the end of the vacation. Vickie had been doting upon the upcoming holistic events and timely workshops. She got butterflies in her stomach, a telltale sign of her rapture, exhilaration, and the anticipation. All of them planned to catch up after Vickie's conference.

"Welcome to the conference. Thanks for the confirmation number, Vickie. Here is your name tag. Plus a special tote for the resonant handouts that you might gather!" the greeter expressed, with an inviting demeanor and a friendly handshake.

"What a beacon of light to begin a holistic summit. My resonance has started at this moment with you, my gift tote, and will continue to fill my day," affirmed Vickie, strolling away to the venues with the diverse speakers and the holistic workshops on a printout. She approached the front rows near the stage and took a middle seat, about twenty minutes ahead of schedule.

"May I sit here? I am *precocious* Amelia. What is your name?" Vickie heard, as she turned quickly, noticing that familiar smile.

"How? What the heck? Are you *really* registered? How about this event *and* our perfect timing? Amelia, how did you even spot me in this almost-full auditorium?" Vickie kept her questions coming, eyes wide-open to seek any clues, a hint, or perhaps, the real mystique of Amelia.

"Hey, we are kindred folks, not just plane buddies. Bionic eyes at the resort entertainment became our well-honed skill. Elton and I wanted you to be surprised, no astounded. Just whenever—our paths crossed at a venue!" Amelia confided, revealing her bright eyes, giving a gentle hug, and patting Vickie's hand. Her spontaneous arrival caused an unmistakable reverberation in Vickie's heart.

"Welcome, *precocious* Amelia. I am *vibrant* Vickie, a kindred persona that wondered if you would ever arrive. You know, several earth angels wanted your seat!" Vickie teased, winking and grinning, only half in jest.

Both of them squeezed and held hands for a minute. Then the lights were dimmed. The waving presenters came to sit down upon the cushioned-lavender chairs placed on mid-stage with a softer lighting.

The renowned and humble professionals were welcomed with applause—the neuroscience-spiritual healer, the psychic medium and meditator, and a metaphysical healer and life coach. Vickie recalled that welcome entry. Extract the messages that resonate in the summit. Already, Vickie felt an inner peace. She listened attentively.

The neuroscience-spiritual healer was at center stage. Place and hold a palm, two or three fingers, or touch your heart gently, taking three purposeful and deeper breaths. Our brain-heart connections, not just our brain. Our research shows that the heart also has phenomenal synapses and a wealth of neurons. Let us make those valued connections happen today.

Raise your consciousness and subconscious awareness. Now, repeat after me. Ask your heart a specific question. Repeat after me.

My heart, what do you want me to know today? What you receive might be shorter—a phrase, a word, certain images, or a spectrum of color. Too long or too much? That is your ego. Just try again...

Amelia and Vickie gave a head nod, knowing that they would dialogue later. More gifts were forthcoming from a psychic medium and meditator. Our loved ones that have died with their messages or signs were astounding. But, it was the closure meditation at this presentation that was unlike others that Vickie had experienced.

We start at your feet, the grounding to Mother Earth. Watch for the colors, the glittering or a diamond-like effect, or a white light. Now, bring that essence up through your toes, the feet, and your ankles. By the time you reach your head, a crowning chakra, capture your feelings or the imagery.

The presenter's voice was mesmerizing in concert with the gentle messages of being safe and going forward. Know that your soul is outside of you, above your crown chakra. In this second, what is your soul asking of you, showing you...

Once again, Vickie and Amelia would stare and nod. They knew. Talk later for sure! The last presenter was a healer and a life coach. Vickie felt a distinct shift in her body, some type of re-alignment. The presenter got up from her lavender-cushioned chair, walking slowly to move toward the center stage.

My colleagues are gifted healers. Now, let us go right to esteemed gifts—the ones that are within your own being. Pick a mantra. Or a familiar mantra that you are using. Important to repeat, as that creates a space and a quietude instead of the random, persistent thoughts. If incessant thoughts appear, watch them float by, forgive them, and just go back to your mantra. Breathe naturally, but deeper.

God, Buddha, ascended masters, team spirits, and different archangels will be with you. Entrust their messages and see their colors or the hues. Go with this resonant ebb and flow—a release of an ego-mind chatter. Keep returning to your mantra to enfold into the peace, soul-fulfillment, and an evolving spirit...

Amelia and Vickie applauded the presenters, holding hands before standing up. Gratitude for a raised consciousness with these presenters was expressed, as they hugged and smiled.

"We have to talk later!" confided Vickie, as she felt glorious with Amelia's vibrant head nods. They needed to make headway through a crowded auditorium to the next venue.

Vickie was happy that she printed the program at home, circling the potential presenters for each day.

The next days of healing modalities and a raised consciousness were enriching and uplifting for the participants. Lively, innovative, and renowned professionals, these globe-trotters for decades or the gifted newcomers, came to share with humanity in their generous, altruistic, and humble ways. Their mind, body, and spirit insights and the current practices were worthy of transport back home for a daily or a weekly renaissance.

Vickie, Amelia, and Elton met again for evening meals and the entertainment. All of them reflected together. What an understatement to say that this Punta Cana resort and a week of eurekas and their good fortune were a treasure.

"So, Amelia relayed my keen interest in next year's conference at Sedona. I would like to integrate the work of these medical intuitives, the holistic doctors, and current practices with my students in adolescent psychology," offered Elton. His energetic spirit interfaced and fused amazingly with Amelia.

"A definite yes—to pursuing the captivating and illusive Sedona. That conference and global presenters will be highlighted at least six months in advance. My dear friend Arlene is coming next year," added Vickie, clasping her hand over her heart.

"Terrific! Hey, how about a little diversion for a bit? I know that you would really enjoy a colleague of mine who will want to participate. Amelia knows him as well. Dale is my colleague and good buddy outside of the university," Elton clarified, as they exchanged intriguing looks with a mention of Vickie's enjoyment of his colleague and good buddy, Dale.

"Why, Elton and Amelia, you are fun and conniving with that look. Are you up to no good or totally interested in my social scene being ramped up?" teased Vickie, as she truly surprised them with her quick observation.

"Why, Vickie, my new and perceptive sidekick, do you think that we are letting you depart without another sense of intrigue beside Sedona?" Amelia quizzed, sharing that look again with Elton, while bending forward to grin and touch Vickie's hand.

"Yeah, call it my sixth sense. I believe that this good buddy named Dale is someone that you want me to meet before Sedona. Am I totally off base or do I have an exquisite perception?" asked Vickie, noting her voice was more enthused than she even expected.

All of them cracked up, knowing the same thoughts were not exclusive to Elton and Amelia in this moment. They made plans to go swimming that day and talk more about Elton's good buddy.

The ocean was inviting. The sun bennies made everyone snooze a bit on their blankets. Somewhere, there was a ringtone of a cell phone.

"Hey, Dale, I was going to call you. Went for a nice swim in this appealing, aquamarine water and crashed on the blanket. Deeper sleep in these bennies, buddy!" added

Elton, getting a kick out of his commentary and whatever responses that Dale was giving in the next minutes.

"Sure, here is Amelia. She is looking mighty fine, a bronzy woman. Her IQ *and* her "EQ" emotional intelligence catapulted beyond both of us at this summit!" Elton touted, giving her a wink and cheek kiss, as she took the phone.

Vickie had drifted off to a dreamscape again. She did not hear them calling her name. Finally, Elton stretched an arm and touched her hand with his phone. She barely opened her eyes.

"Hey, Dale. She was dreaming of her mermaid swim. She can chat in a few seconds. You take care and see you soon, buddy!"

Elton's phone was in Vickie's hand. Elton and Amelia were motioning to talk. My word, she was barely awake.

"Hi Dale! Well, I heard about you, but Elton and Amelia are holding back the real stories until this evening at dinner," Vickie joked, wondering how she awakened so quickly. After the call, a few thoughts percolated.

Incredible. We talked, enjoyed, and even bantered longer than a few minutes.

Dale was intrigued about the conference highlights and responded how they might be integrated with the students in adolescent psychology. Dale's voice had a deeper resonance, his spirit seemed vibrant, and his witty asides kept the charmed duo chatting longer than expected. Dale offered an idea for a foursome get-together after Punta Cana.

"Sure! I shall share that idea during our swims at this Paradiso. Beaming our glorious weather and images of this aquamarine ocean. Quite intriguing to talk, Dale. Be well and enjoy the rest of the week," expressed Vickie, revealing an appealing voice that even made her pause and wonder.

Vickie had a walloping grin, handing the phone to Elton, but not saying peep about Dale's idea. Vickie guessed that they were eavesdropping. The wanna-go-swimming invitation happened, topped off with their peals of laughter, gentle hand-holding, and dashing off to the enchanting ocean with the undulating waves. Vickie's inner thoughts began to percolate again.

Earth to Vickie... Keep that enthusiastic attitude and let the positive vibes percolate. It has been awhile since my singles groups and those meet-ups. Dale's invitation and our dialogues will happen after my return and settling down at home. I need to pause and wonder for a few minutes. It is high time.

Vickie swam back to the shoreline and dashed again toward the appealing ocean, diving into a perfect wave. She popped up, incredibly refreshed. Vickie beamed at this lush junction of the Atlantic and Caribbean waters.

Ah, there were Elton and Amelia swimming her way...

Elton and Amelia arrive in a distant place and mystical time,

Soulful connections with Dale, refreshing and unexpected,

The pinnacles of Vickie's healing summit arrive on a timely cue...

Scents of Cedar And Pine

Aromatic scents of the cedar and pine trees lingered from a morning rain mist. Abby stretched out on a cushy lounge chair under her covered balcony to view the conservation land. She knew.

Breathe in the alchemy of the cedar and pine trees. Slow down her breaths.

Closing her eyes slowly, Abby imagined a night train to the vibrant stars and a waxing moon. This night-bound moonscape, its inescapable life force, continued to transform the morning with a recharging.

Each day enlightened Abby's evolving practice. She drew upon her imagination, creative imaging, and experienced a replenishment.

Abby grew fond of this tranquil state with her soft murmurs of real appreciation, unconditional love, a compassion, and her gratitude. Then she scribed in a daily journal, aware that selective words about these moments were always more powerful than a distant memory.

The imagined vapors of the divine and the undulating pulses of energy, like my tingles or chills, are no longer surreal. A small jerk in my arms and shoulders and those glorious hues of color appear. Purple, gold, and emerald green this morning.

My written words or phrases for today. Believe. Entrust the rest is coming. Always make the choice of hope over despair. Today, there is a golden abundance with my reappearing 11:11 on the clock or any multiples of seven and three.

All remain my telltale signs. Thank you Green Tara and my Archangel Uriel.

This morning, I honor each of you holding a space, the guidance for myself and our world. I am worthy, receiving the unconditional care and a compassion.

Whenever my mind chatter creates an uncertainty or the angst, I ask for a clearing of the negative vibrations, my worrisome scenarios, or the unworthy thoughts.

I honor and permit these light-filling releases. I am receptive. I am grateful to channel the highest good for myself and for our world.

As she dated and penned in her journal, Abby still smelled the scent of cedar and pine. She drifted into this particular re-awakening this morning. An utmost caring and a compassion were felt in the deepest chambers of her heart.

The experience of joy with an evolving solace was being imprinted from last evening and this morning. Abby placed her petite hands of appreciation over her slower heartbeats.

Suddenly, she felt compelled. Abby strolled off her balcony towards that lingering scent, an alchemy of the cedars and tall pines.

Trusting the imprints from last evening and this morning,

An alchemy of the cedar and pine trees,

Completion of Abby's nature walks, breathing deeply of that essence...

HAPPY
THOUGHTS

Giggling Ms. Doogle and Dr. Holliday in the too-quiet library,

Ding-a-lings, valued conversations, and the tosh moments,

Cheerio, Ms. Doogle...

Cheerio, Ms. Doogle

The head librarian forged ahead with a plan. The agent was in Dallas, not in New York, Los Angeles, or Chicago. Her demeanor and British accent seemed to coax the favorable and charming dialogues, regardless of the occasion or even a controversial concern. Ms. Doogle reflected during the phone rings.

Too many ding-a-lings. No protege or apprentice staff for the actual agent? Blimey, I need to compose myself. Promptly, this second!

"Good afternoon, this is Ms. Doogle at University of Texas, our Denton campus. A teacher has emerged as a gifted Assistant Professor, given a trade book that complements her educational psychology textbook. Blimey, look at her book, I have touted to numerous colleagues! Already selling to mass audiences, just with our student grapevine. I saw her in our library, so I decided to ring you up. Call me audacious or quite daft at my stage in life, but this telly was worth a gamble. She believes that *only* full professors are the cat's meow. Tosh! Might I text Dr. Holliday to come to my desk for a bit of a chat?" Ms. Doogle queried, in a melodic voice with her arresting, sensational Brit accent.

Ms. Doogle set the silver-rimmed glasses down on her slim nose, giving the tally-ho wave. Stepping closer to the desk, she overheard that Dr. Holliday was coming. Ms. Doogle put a long, slender finger to her pursed lips in a sh-h-h motion, pointing to a nearby chair. She handed over her phone, but only after a signature sign-off.

"Ms. Rebecca MacDonald, here is the lauded Dr. Holliday, for whom I have utmost regard. My *dearest appreciation* for your precious, respected time," Ms. Doogle affirmed, still exuding that brilliant British accent.

"Hello, Ms. MacDonald! Ms. Doogle texted me that a respected agent was on her phone, willing to speak about my trade book. How kind of you to chat with me!" conveyed Dr. Holliday, in a grateful and very enthusiastic voice.

"Tease me with a few morsels about your trade book, like where it is selling beyond academia and one compelling idea for its next debut," she responded, in a light-hearted but a precise, professional manner about the exact morsels to offer.

Their conversation lasted an unforeseen and incredible forty minutes. Again, Ms. Rebecca MacDonald conveyed the suitable items for Saturday's appointment. The Dallas office would be low key with no staff, her distinct preference with a Saturday meet-up.

After this unanticipated dialogue, Dr. Holliday sprang up from the chair, clutching Ms. Doogle's portable land-line phone and her cell phone in two, tremoring hands. Wow, she was boot-scootin' around that massive desk in mere seconds.

"How can I *ever* thank you? Thanks sounds so trite. I had no spunk or even an ounce of bravura skill. So, you glanced at our literary reference, tagging a Dallas agent in nothing flat. Indeed, you even pointed out where to eavesdrop with your call. Oh, I adore you!" confessed Dr. Holliday, hugging the charmed and giggling Ms. Doogle.

"You must know by now, my dear! I am smitten with your student rapport and giving me the opportune sessions to share the divine secrets in our library. I have admired your upsurge to acclaim, Dr. Holliday, and your down-to-earth and whimsical personality. You should have surmised that I would ring up an agent in a jiff," Ms. Doogle continued to profess, sighing contentedly with her aftermath emotions and the "posh outcomes" of their afternoon's glory.

Dr. Holliday felt like a floating soul. She left the library and drifted across the campus to her office. This Saturday appointment, a verified literary agent, and the nearby Dallas office—only three days away—were beyond astounding.

Ms. Doogle and Dr. Holliday were privy, but no one else. That evening and the next morning, she felt the urge to murmur aloud. Esme felt that a guardian angel or her spirit team were still listening.

Friday evening and I do not feel sleepy. Our elevated and remarkable afternoon still feels real and surreal. I am packed with a tote for Ms. Rebecca, full of my treasures. Hope floats with my anticipation.

Hey, I must have slept. The alarm is going off and my beloved phone confirms that today is indeed Saturday. Onward and bolt outta here, Dr. Esme Holliday.

Wow, smooth as silk. The Dallas office was an easy find. Ms. Rebecca MacDonald said that Saturday would be low key.

One car and mine equals only two autos. Guess any proteges and the literary staff did not sleep overnight! Stop laughing, Esme, and park your car near the entry door.

Ms. Rebecca MacDonald, Literary Agent was listed on the panel beside the number seven. Esme pressed that button, opened the buzzing door, and rode up on the empty elevator. Esme followed the arrows pointing to the direction of her office.

"Ms. Rebecca MacDonald? First and foremost, thank you for this Saturday appointment. Here is a favorite tote with my hopeful treasures, only filled with what you requested," Esme announced, grinning and extending her hand to greet Ms. Rebecca's firm handshake.

"I like the quiet of Saturdays. Thought it might be good for you, the green Assistant Prof, so I heard through the British grapevine. Pull up that cushy chair and show me your hopeful treasures," Ms. Rebecca suggested, noticing Esme's scan of her topsy-turvy bookshelves, chock-full of diverse genres and the notable authors.

Dr. Holliday handed over the trade book and a two-page letter from a husband-wife literary team in New York. They debated about Dr. Holliday as a potential and upcoming author, even with a substantial schedule and their high-profile authors. Yes, it was a rejection letter, but the context was empathic and very encouraging.

"First of all, please call me Rebecca. How about you, Dr. Holliday?" she quizzed, peering over her reading glasses with a whimsical smirk.

"Esme!"

"Terrific. Now, let me take a peek at these hopeful treasures, as you have remarked. Hmm, feel free to browse those topsy-turvy bookshelves as I read," Rebecca offered, gazing momentarily at this funky-dressed and younger person, prior to skimming through Esme's trade book and a rejection letter from the duo-teamed New York agency.

The day morphed into the late evening. Rebecca shared immediately. Esme's trade book had potential, but her rejection letter was the creme' de creme' for sure. Why?

Busy, credible agents did not have time to write a two-page *and* a single-spaced letter about their debates. Or offer any apologies for being busy with the already-published authors. Or offer any specific reasons for their encouragements.

Their letter reaffirmed that Esme was a potential talent and the so-called package in the industry. She also appeared to be an unwavering individual who needed to keep searching for a literary agent.

Rebecca never accepted Esme's checks. Saturday meetings happened for at least a year, while Esme pursued her university career. Grabbing a book, reading passages to Esme, teaching about how to elevate trade book writings, and top-shelf hints to digest happened steadily. Then came that different Saturday meet-up. There was a request to teach elsewhere—somewhere prestigious to enhance Esme's credentials.

"Rebecca, you are privy. There are no hush-hush stories between us. I love my university, the inspiring colleagues, and a diversity of students. I am not leaving for any lofty academia that I witness from my renowned faculty and networking at our national conferences. But, I am willing to seek and secure that prestige-status gig and a summer session for your industry," reaffirmed Esme. Rebecca accepted Esme's determined spirit, a valued career, and what not to give up, while blossoming and vying for a biggie-sized publishing quest.

"Where have you mulled over, contemplated, or want to propose, my dear friend?" Rebecca questioned, showing her quirky smile, particularly when feisty Esme talked so passionately.

"An Ivy League college in suburban Boston!" Esme chimed, full of tenacity and her melodic exuberance.

"Do it, my dear. Interview. You will snag a distinguished and respected summer position," Rebecca encouraged, letting Esme surmise that her choice of a stellar college was a radiant *and* green light.

During the spring semester, Esme had been roused and supported to put forth a portfolio for an early promotion to full professor. She had interviewed for the heralded summer position, but requested the Associate Professor level.

During the past summers, their faculty hired an adjunct or the Assistant Professor. When the Department Chair called, Esme was the finalist and offered a "Visiting Associate" status. That new decision was a definite surprise.

Behind closed doors, that new choice probably set a higher bar for Esme. Her own faculty and administration were very impressed. Rebecca and Esme were thrilled. Rebecca was also flying high.

"Rebecca, the visionary joy happened. Your new author received a six-figure advance, regardless of your claim—not in the New York circle of literary agents. Super kudos, Rebecca. Your exceptional talent, an exclusive effort, and the ultimate success did happen. What a well-deserved honor!" bragged Esme, adoring their mutual hugs and clapping like the little kiddos.

Life went forward on the fast track. Esme received the rave reviews and was invited to return the next summer. The sterling accolade, however, was an early promotion to full professorship at her cherished university.

Rebecca was also pushing for the mountain tops. Esme was moonlighting with trade book endeavors, becoming the two-career person. Juggling all of the balls in the air lasted another two years. Inevitably, the time for a decision barged onto the scene.

"Rebecca, I am at the crossroads with these passionate career paths. My health and well being are compromised. I must decide. My new promotion and everything that entails at my endearing university? Or our wondrous years and your pitches for my book, the next books, and a commitment to tour and promote the whole shebang?" Esme questioned earnestly, aware of Rebecca's enormous efforts and their precious years of an evolving friendship.

"Esme, it is your showdown and a choice. I want you to leave academia for this potential career. Just teach as an adjunct at your university or during the summertime near Boston again," Rebecca suggested.

"Dearest Rebecca, I would not make enough dinero to pay my weekly or the monthly expenses. I am frugal, but my esteemed academia pays a monthly salary and my multifaceted benefits. Plus, it never has been just a job. I still have no advance for this book, never mind any future books. My professional and heartfelt choice is to stay in academia. I shall pursue my trade book market, but mostly on semester breaks and exclude the distractions of any summer teaching," Esme elaborated, revealing her tearful eyes and a compassionate intonation.

"Esme, I wish you the best. You know I care about you, professionally and personally. This business is tough, even tougher to predict. The best-selling authors get the big kahuna advances, a film spin-off, the product endorsements, and whatever. I shall still be here for you, whenever your book revisions happen. I know how to pitch your creativity and a grand finale. And, any equally delightful books to follow," Rebecca offered, revealing an emotive and raspy voice while they clinched in a colossal hug.

The next year was busy. Rebecca's author with a six-figure advance was receiving attractive film bids. Esme loved her full professorship. For newbie Assistant profs—the rookies—she became a sought-after mentor. Semester breaks and her entire summers were devoted to trade book endeavors for Rebecca. They talked regularly, grabbed a coffee, or enjoyed the divine eateries, usually when Esme was consulting near the Turtle Creek splendor of Dallas.

Esme headed to beguiling Geneseo in upstate New York for half of the next summer. Her charming and witty parents had died a couple of years ago, but their homestead was "a keeper" for her older brother, Joseph.

Both siblings enjoyed an affectionate bond since childhood and throughout any lifespan melodramas. Nowadays, they snatched a seasonal or the opportune reunions, enriching those entertaining days or fabulous weeks squeezed in between Joseph's clients and Esme's trade book writings.

"Joseph, I am going for a luxurious swim at the lake. Taking a picnic, too. Be back for dinner. Let's make something wicked yummy! Have my phone and will check periodically, my dear bro," Esme disclosed, blowing her theatrical, airborne kisses to display a playful affection and then watching for Joseph's cool, fetching grin.

"Hey, enjoy sis! Have a couple of clients interested in our lake properties. Maybe we will chat, if they want to walk the shoreline near our beach and the park. Be wicked charming! Esme, you get a partial commission, if they buy a lake home!" Joseph teased, revealing those blue-blue and twinkling eyes just like witty Dad.

Esme adored his quaint Geneseo home in the spring, summer, and fall seasons, never during the chill-ya-to-the-bone winters. Today, she swam a lot. Then she devoured the granola and mixed fruits in her Greek yogurt concoction.

Esme took a refreshing cat nap. After a longer and relaxing swim, she stretched across a fluffy blanket, peered into a beach tote, and pulled out her phone. Yay, no texts or the voicemails. Something in that exact moment made her sit up to call Rebecca.

"Sorry, this is not a working number," Esme heard after a few ring tones.

"I shall try again," she mumbled to her cell phone, only to hear the same message.

At dinner, Esme told Joseph about the message. He suggested that Rebecca might have changed a personal number, but probably not the office phone. Yes, of course, Joseph offered a perceptive insight. Esme would try the office phone in the morning.

Both of them devoured the grilled salmon, the brown rice, and a veggie medley. There was a rousing toast with a fine wine—to Joseph's two clients that purchased the lake bungalows and Esme's full professorship, her covenant for an intriguing safari.

"Sunset on your incredible deck and a limoncello gelato, Joseph. We are living to the hilt!" Esme broadcasted, raising her cordial glass to click again with Joseph's outstretched hand.

"Indeed! Our vibrant, fun-loving souls and my lucky star for your extended visit. Always, the best-ever reunions!" Joseph chimed, as their next cha-ching with his vintage glasses topped off a spectacular sunset.

The next week passed too quickly. Esme got numerous busy signals on Rebecca's office phone, lessening her former twinges of angst. As her brother drove to the airport, they made the captivating plans for his "top notch visit" the following month.

Esme had quality time to accomplish her book tweaks for Rebecca during the next week. The summer months in north central Texas were much warmer than upstate New York. Outdoor swimming during the morning or in the late afternoon were relaxing rituals along with a daily walkabout at a nearby lake park. Meanwhile, Esme was truly looking forward to tomorrow.

Off to Dallas—dazzling Big D—for an engaging luncheon with longtime colleagues that lived in the suburbs closer to the city. By mid-afternoon, Esme planned to drop off her book tweaks for Rebecca. She parked the car and got into the building without buzzing, as a man waited to hold the door for Esme's entry. At the office door, there was a sign: For Lease.

"Oh, my goodness! What is *happening*, Rebecca?" gasped Esme out loud, unaware that the man at the entry was also on the same floor.

"Are you looking for Ms. Rebecca MacDonald, the literary agent?" he inquired, a booming voice emanating down the hall.

"Oh, dear... Yeah, I am," Esme managed to reply, not sure who was talking, until she turned and saw the same man who was at the entry door.

"I am sorry. Ms. MacDonald died about two months ago. I just met her boyfriend, as he was moving out with many boxes of books and putting up the lease sign. I am terribly sorry," he repeated slowly in a kind voice, not even knowing about a precious friendship or their writer-agent wayfaring.

Esme whispered a faint thanks, but had to leave quickly. Somehow, she drove to a smaller plaza down the road, while the tears streamed down her cheeks. Esme parked and started to writhe with her sobs. Finally, she drove back from the city. At home, Esme called Joseph.

"Oh, sis! Oh no, I am so sorry. Um-m, listen... Listen, we are going to locate someone who knew Rebecca and her boyfriend. I was coming your way, but I am coming pronto.

Please, try to... Oh, heck, try to rest, if you can. I am sending my hugs. Dear Esme, we experienced such mourning with the deaths of our parents and our significant friends. Take time for mourning and healing, Esme," he expressed gently.

Joseph packed, booked a flight, and found the literary agents located in Dallas. He recalled Rebecca's successful author, so he tracked down the publisher. In a day, Joseph found Rebecca's boyfriend with a senior editor's guidance. This kind editor heard Rebecca's forecasts. Esme was her "acclaimed professor and writer that would land a hefty advance from a publisher—soon."

When he arrived in two days, Joseph held Esme in a gentle, swaying embrace as she sobbed, not caring about the bustling airport terminal or any walkways. Finally, with their supportive arms intertwined, both of them walked slowly to Esme's car in a parking garage. Only then did Joseph begin to share his anecdotes about the publisher and what a senior editor knew about Rebecca's boyfriend.

"Rebecca's boyfriend sent you a letter in care of Ms. Doogle at the university. He heard the earlier stories about the evolving Saturdays for a few years. Rebecca updated him that you were spending most of the summer on the East coast with a close brother and writing for her. Undoubtedly, that letter is with Ms. Doogle," Joseph replied confidently, giving Esme another embrace.

"Oh, Ms. Doogle has retired. I was hoping to visit her before my trip to Geneseo. No summer sessions, just the book for Rebecca. A colleague left a voicemail when I was at your homestead, relaying that Ms. Doogle was showing signs of dementia. Oh, my bright and charming Brit librarian and friend was fading into that insidious dis-ease. We shall never forget our Mom's declines. Joseph, I need to visit Ms. Doogle, if we can..." began Esme with tearful eyes and a tremor in her voice.

"Of course, we shall visit. Just give me that colleague's number. Both of us will figure out the best time tomorrow or the next day. Right now? You rest, my dear sis," Joseph intoned softly, never withholding his compassionate, giving nature.

"I am so relieved. Grateful that you are here, sweet Joseph. Our love and heart are always in sync. I shall relax for a spell, but I want to visit our outdoor market in the downtown square. We need a plentiful meal. I have not eaten much. You probably have not eaten well, given *all* that you have accomplished in two days!" expressed Esme, her eyes brimming and the heartfelt tears streaming down her high-boned and classic cheeks.

"Go veggie out, my deserving sis. I am going to catch up on my clients. Remember? Do not forget your commission. The client that I brought to the beach did purchase a lakefront home, given your positive vibes! Hopefully, two clients will also buy on the lake with my return calls," Joseph declared, flashing a thumbs up sign and his huge grin, noting a beginning shift of Esme's energy on this valued afternoon.

Esme took a longer cat nap. They scurried to the outdoor market, bringing home a plentiful wicker basket. As they cooked dinner, the talks switched to his clients. Talented Joseph did his magic with the two lakefront deals. Her colleague called back, updating Joseph that tomorrow after lunch was fine for visiting Ms. Doogle.

"Thanks for driving! Not sure what to expect, but we were Mom's advocates and beloved caregivers throughout her dementia and the Alzheimer's declines. Look Joseph, here is Ms Doogle's bungalow," commented Esme, as she pointed to a lovely abode.

"Nice! Fits your stories. In London, closer to the Kensington Park, there are quaint residences like her bungalow. Esme, let us pause to hope for Ms. Doogle's moments of clarity..." he offered, not finishing his sentence as they held hands, strolling towards a beautiful oak door and ringing a charming bell.

"Hello...hello. Come for a visit?" Ms. Doogle asked, glancing momentarily at Joseph, but staring at Esme and giving a slight smile.

"Ms. Doogle, you are the best! I am still your acclaimed Esme at our university. You made that first call to my agent, Ms. Rebecca. I have been traveling to visit my brother, Joseph!" Esme revealed, filling up the possible blanks and interlacing an arm with her brother. Joseph's immediate head nods and a kindly handshake helped.

"Hmm, Esme... Oh yes, Esme. A visit with your brother. Your brother?" Ms. Doogle repeated, looking a bit vacant for a few seconds.

"Yes, indeed. My favorite and only brother!" Esme pronounced, delighted when both of them began to laugh, as they did in the library where "quiet and only a few whispers" were the supposed conduct.

Ms. Doogle offered them tea, not the high tea, as she did for many years. They chatted casually. Esme mentioned Rebecca, their visits, and a letter that was sent while Esme was visiting her brother.

"My colleague thought that letter was sent in care of you. I was staying with my brother most of the summer. Do you recall any letter?" asked Esme, in a gentle manner.

"Oh, dear. I have mail? Let me look here...no here. Perhaps, in the kitchen cupboard," she said, wandering off and returning with her unopened mail. Ms. Doogle handed that stack to Esme and Joseph seated on her couch.

The unopened letter was there, in care of Ms. Doogle. Esme and Joseph exchanged a quick glance, but pretended to examine the entire stack. Ms. Doogle sat in a tall chair nearby.

"I think we saw the letter, but let me double-check with Joseph. Yes, here it is. Not opened, but it was addressed to Esme in care of you, Ms. Doogle," restated Esme, showing her the envelope.

"Oh, I put that stack in a kitchen cupboard. Forgot. I am getting forgetful, I think," Ms. Doogle commented, looking at them.

"You knew about Rebecca, our friendship, and my book writing. I can open it now.

Why not?" Esme offered, pretending it was just a letter from Rebecca while she was traveling.

Ms. Doogle was looking tired and a bit worried, but agreed with Esme. As Esme read the letter from Rebecca's boyfriend, she started to wipe the tears from her cheeks. Joseph put his arm around Esme's shoulders, reading the paragraphs.

Rebecca's death was quick, a relentless pancreatic cancer. Rebecca's boyfriend was shocked and grief-stricken, so heading back to Colorado with his family and old friends was a quick decision. He remembered the stories of Ms. Doogle and Esme, so he wrote what he could in those difficult moments, mailing that letter in care of Ms. Doogle.

"Ms. Doogle, come sit with us on the couch—right here with Joseph and I. I want to share why I was crying. Please, come sit with us," Esme gestured, revealing her empathic voice.

Ms. Doogle sat in the middle of them, exactly where Esme had patted on the couch. Ms. Doogle listened to Esme share that Rebecca died of pancreatic cancer. She would not recall the details, but Ms. Doogle knew today's moment and became crestfallen.

Ms. Doogle needed to open this letter, but she put it with a stack in the kitchen cupboard. The accumulating pile was not apparent on a counter or a table, so Rebecca's letter and other mail items were forgotten.

All of them squeezed hands on the small couch, letting Ms. Doogle's awareness, their visit, and the companionship of today become a comfort. After ten minutes, Ms. Doogle sighed and looked longingly at Esme.

"My sweet, I want you to rest, perhaps a short nap? Joseph will return with our yummy food. We can have dinner together. I am going to rest on your couch. How does that sound, Ms. Doogle?" Esme asked slowly, squeezing her slender hand again and giving her a comforting hug.

"I...I would like you to stay. Dinner is nice. I can nap now," Ms. Doogle confided, squeezing Esme's hand, standing up, and walking slowly to a bedroom down the hallway.

Esme was stronger than she envisioned with this visit. She sat on the couch, not napping but preferring to daydream about the special years with endearing Rebecca. Rebecca and Esme became the dynamic duo, as proclaimed by their passionate colleagues and their close friends.

Joseph felt that Esme would prefer to stay at the quaint bungalow. Both of them needed a respite. The town market was a pleasant atmosphere, easy to shop and check out without much fanfare. Making dinner and taking this private time were prime examples of his sister's loving-kind demeanor—toward herself and for Ms. Doogle. Joseph knew his sister appreciated his shopping spree and his time alone. He was back in an hour, surprised to notice Esme on the same couch, looking ever so peaceful.

"Joseph, thanks for understanding and shopping. I was daydreaming of all of our special times, the crazy-good vibes. A peacefulness settled in my inner being the entire time. Ms. Doogle needed a longer cat nap. I shall get started with dinner. Why don't you relax instead of helping me cook, although we love our kitchen playtime," teased Esme.

"Nope, I relaxed at your pleasant market and my shopping spree. We are always ready to cook and play in the kitchen. The aromatics will wake up Ms. Doogle. Maybe we can peek in the cupboards for dinnerware and perhaps, find a bit more of the lost-and-found surprises," Joseph teased, making Esme giggle in those memorable minutes.

Ms. Doogle did wake up to the yummy aromas of a promised dinner. She looked better and still had a relative clarity as they enjoyed a healthy, scrumptious meal.

Illusive dementia was definitely sneaking into Ms. Doogle's life. There were no Brit quips or her expressive language. There was her unopened mail in an obscure kitchen cupboard. A vacantness on this supposed good or better day was apparent, throughout this afternoon and during their dinner.

"Well, I can visit next week. Would you adore my company? Another bonus of a yummy dinner?" Esme inquired, enticing Ms. Doogle with twinkling eyes and the gentle pats to her slender hand.

"Oh…oh, yes!" Ms. Doogle expressed, in a melodic voice that was heard for the first time since their arrival at the quaint bungalow.

Joseph flew back home during that week. The weeks passed, as Esme kept up the promised visits and the yummy dinners. She spoke regularly with Joseph, keeping him apprized of Ms. Doogle's dementia. They were more sales of his prime lake properties. They also chatted about Esme's serene reflections of Rebecca and a grandiose finale with the trade book.

"Joseph, I do not know what to do with this book, regarding an agent. Rebecca was unique, never part of that clique of New York literary agents. But, I get those intuitive vibes that something will work. Soon… Truly not questioning my intuition or that mystique," Esme reflected, giving time for her perceptive brother to interject his take on an agent.

"Why don't you call the publisher with Rebecca's new author and her big kahuna advance? The editorial staff might know of someone? Another crazy-good agent that Rebecca would endorse for Esme," Joseph offered, sounding quite credible with that suggestion.

On their next conversation, Esme relayed her call to the publisher. Joseph noted her cocked head and confident smile in a nanosecond. Before he could ask, she said there was another crazy-good agent. Apparently, Rebecca talked about this agent with the editorial staff, highlighting that Esme was the next keeper. The senior editors recalled Rebecca's teasing—if I should die before waking up tomorrow, be sure to give him a jingle for my gemstone, Esme.

"Guess what his name is?" Esme tantalized, giving a funny grin, a jive dance, and a thumb-up sign.

"There is no way, Esme! Not Joseph!" he declared, starting to belly laugh.

"My sweet brother, you are a genius! Guess what else? I am meeting him tomorrow, as this special Joseph has read the *grand finale* of my trade book!"

"I have got goose bumps, sis! I get this guy—Joseph II—is the real deal, like crazy-good Rebecca. Why not? His name is Joseph!" he touted, flashing his supportive grin and noticing Esme's exuberant facial expressions.

"Tune in, my loving and very supportive brother. Hey, bro'... I shall FaceTime again!"

The drive to Dallas was easy. The agent's office was past the old plaza where Esme had parked and sobbed with the news of Rebecca's death. It was a Saturday appointment for a quieter meet-up and their discussions.

Buzzing into the building, Esme went up the elevator to the third floor. Office number seven to the right. Joseph's door was ajar. His reading glasses were perched on his nose, a pen tapping slowly on a last page of Esme's book.

"Excuse me, I am Esme. We had our appointment today..." she began, only to be interrupted with an enthused head nod and his beckoning gesture.

"Please, Esme—sit close by—at my grandmother's chair. No kidding! Pretty great shape, eh? Well, I was rereading the last two pages before you arrived, lost in the universe," he added, watching Esme's eyes, viewing his book titles as she meandered around a nearby table.

Silence. They looked at each other for a few seconds. Joseph gave a super handshake. Esme smiled, feeling her goose bumps and a nervous excitement, but kept a suave-cool look.

"Esme, I am going to cut to the chase. On Rebecca's behalf and her delightful craziness, she was perceptive. Plain and simple, I want to be your agent. Your book needs the tweaking, but it is worth a pitch to a top notch publisher. A sure thing—on me as your agent and the ride of a lifetime, Esme?" Joseph requested, full of charismatic appeals and a distinctive moxie.

"Amazing! I am astounded and taken off guard. Almost surreal moments for me, I confess. However, I must ask about my professorship journey and writing on breaks, summers, and whenever else I can. Rebecca knew my academe passion as well as going ahead with a trade book...", she started to exclaim, not able to finish her thoughts.

"Respectfully, may I interrupt? Endearing Rebecca and I schmoozed about new clients and their potential books, the tours, and the whole package," he confessed, still revealing a charisma. "We shall figure out your life's safari, I promise," reassured Joseph, feeling Esme's wise eyes looking right into his being.

"I am honored and accept! Joseph, you are the next keeper of my radiant light in an indigenous industry of the unbridled literary agents. My *earth angel,* I promise to keep you apprized of my synchronistic and avant-garde life balance," Esme declared confidently. She paused to reach over and touch his hand for a few seconds.

"Rest assured, I cherish your promise," Esme affirmed, exuding an authenticity. Her wise eyes reappeared.

Joseph knew. He would never forget his promise.

Journeys to the epicenter of Esme's heart,

Devotions, the losses and mournings, and her unbridled hopes,

New promises appear on Esme and Joseph's vast horizon...

Loss of beautiful Patrick encased Farah's thoughts,

Moving ahead with life's twists and turns, her carousel, and an unforeseen and companionate caring,

Delays. Never the denials...

Delays Never Denials

Farah decided. It was exactly three days after ringing in a new year. Fifteen years ago, the pancreatic cancer hit with a vengeance. Her older brother's death at fifty-five was never expected, still a surreal memory for Farah.

"It is your *GARNET* birthday. Let's boogie-woogie again, Patrick. You were the superstar dancer," declared Farah. She continued to talk aloud, recalling his lovely personality. "This venue features a super band, Patrick. Alas, no DJ's!"

After dinner, Farah cruised to the dance venue in her baby-blue Porsche 911. Patrick gifted Farah his classic car. She idolized every occasion and the incredible moments of cruising.

At the bar, Farah ordered a beer. She raised a frosted glass to the full moon and murmured softly.

"It is a super moon, Patrick. 'Tis a fabulous eve for your January 4th birthday!" Then she waved at the bartender.

"A couple of orange slices, please?" Farah queried, in her beguiling voice.

Sebastian, the handsome bartender, gave a smile and winked. "Sure!"

Farah flashed her pearly whites—a translucent, engaging smile—right back. She knew that Sebastian noticed her vibe. The oranges hit the spot as Farah let a reflective musing return.

Well, Patrick. It is an interesting venue. Sebastian, my handsome and likable bartender, keeps returning to chit-chat, grin, and wink at me. The music is superb, our definite style of boogie-woogie. Hmm, the chance of potential prospects—who knows, my endearing Patrick?

Still sipping her frosted glass of beer, Farah was tapped gently on an already bronzy-tan shoulder. She turned slowly to witness a wicked handsome guy, his stylish duds, and the most stunning of all—his salt-and-pepper gray hair. He started to move closer to Farah's bar stool.

"Do you mind if I sit here to buy a drink?" he requested, with a cute half-smile.

"Not at all. Go for it," Farah offered, revealing her appealing cadence and a spontaneous, fabulous smile.

Sebastian served his beer, a bit tipsy with the bottle. He swept up the beer bottle in the nick of time. There were cheers from the bystanders and a quickie apology from Sebastian—before he fled the scene.

He turned to Farah again with a cordial grin. "Well, good evening! My name is Dillon."

Oh heck, what a connection! Too fast for me. Dillon's striking blue eyes are like gargantuan doors to a kinder soul, Patrick. Too soon for me…

"Indeed, a grand evening, Dillon," she managed to reply, noting that he remained seated on the bar stool. "My name is Farah." He kept an exquisite eye contact the entire evening.

Dance spirits. Dillon was different. Their dialogues were easy, so natural. Her inner muse began to interrupt.

Boogie-woogie. Yay, the band hype limits any of the up-close and slow dancing, Patrick! I like Dillon, but I am here for only five months. Snowbird, I am! Wait a minute. My telepathic messages are being interrupted by Dillon.

"I am enjoying this eve. I have dated. Longer marriage, but not a nightmare divorce. Hmm, about ten years ago. You are definitely an intelligent and a joyous individual with a splendid attitude," Dillon shared.

"Thanks for those compliments, Dillon. I do have an attitude *and* an altitude to boot! I am enjoying this evening as well. I liked this dance venue last year and this disco-pop band. They are quite talented."

"Last year? How did I miss you?" Dillon wondered. His remarks seemed authentic, like his avant-garde style and a lively spirit. Farah took note.

Snowbird or not, Dillon seemed rather interested. They danced and talked until the end of the band's gig. During a break, Farah confirmed another venue for the band.

"Maybe we shall see each other at that venue, if you are going?" Dillon asked, staring back at her with those Caribbean-blue, sparkling eyes. He started a half-grin again, causing her muse to pop up.

Darn, Patrick. Never mind our instant connection. It is just too soon. On and off, on and off. I just got off a crazy merry-go-round back home. Oh, I truly need a better focus, Patrick.

"Well, I arrived here about two weeks ago. I shall probably go to that new venue," Farah admitted, maintaining her direct eye contact.

"Fantastic. Perhaps, another dance? I have an early and busy day with my corporate meetings and a team of lawyers, so I need to leave when the venue is over," Dillon added, still looking interested. There were more intervening thoughts for Farah.

Too charming, Patrick? Definitely a fabulous eve, but no jumping on my carousel too fast. Damn, I feel a mellowing and my compassionate vibes. I already know that I am going to that new dance venue.

January, February, March, April, and the merry month of May. Trust. Dialogues.

Stellar dance venues, swimming together at the ocean, and such creative, engaging storytelling at the local gigs. Their travels to the eclectic festivals or the farmers markets around the entire state were during the week days.

Weekends became the opportune cruises to Saint Martin and Bermuda. They were a couple who remained intrigued across the five months.

"We need to pause. Slow down," Farah was saying, as she touched Dillon's arm tenderly. "I am a snowbird and will definitely head home..." she began, for the hundredth or the millionth time.

Dillon kept listening to Farah's intonation with a lovely expression. Her unmistakable laughs and a joyous face would happen soon.

His ruckus laughs came forth immediately. Both of them were belly laughing again. Farah thought of her intriguing flashbacks, especially when they were so enamored.

My daily reminders and the vibrant memories return, Patrick. I know our words, almost verbatim. Darlin' diva, you are the ever-sweet Farah. Just like your mystical book—but, a very daring diva. Then it is my impassioned moment. My sweet thang, Dillon, you are incredibly caring, compassionate, a diehard romantic, and a definite charmer.

Captivating laughs, split-second moments of spontaneity, and the smashing playtime—just like uninhibited kiddos. Their mutual bravado appeared at the first dance venue. Packing in the adventures, a living-large style, and the mutual storytelling gigs came naturally across the five months. Farah knew the clock was ticking away and began to contemplate.

It is later in life for us, Patrick. Dillon and I are revisiting an unconditional love, a trust, and the new beginnings. Only two weeks left—before I head back home. Oh, Patrick, I want to... Wait, Dillon is hugging and talking to me at the same time. Gotta go!

"It is mind-boggling and overwhelming, yet what we know at this very moment. Only FaceTime on phone calls? Emails and only our texts? What months and weeks can I fly to your home? Be with you again, Farah?"

"Oh, I never expected these unique months. I am overwhelmed and grateful, my kindred friend and my loving spirit. Dillon, you know that you have an open invitation."

Farah knew that Patrick was a rare individual, not just her perceptive brother. She knew that divine Patrick would accept her heartfelt feelings across the five months. Her reflections returned effortlessly.

Our realities are emotionally-charged. Both of us are still transitioning in our life journey. Only five months! I know what you are thinking and probably semi-worrying about me, Patrick.

Yes, I am back on that carousel, but my choice is purposeful. You understand who I am and love me unconditionally, even in a heavenly bliss. I yearn to stay connected with Dillon and our new beginnings.

My loving brother, Patrick... Oh, I miss you terribly.

Farah's flashbacks with a heartfelt presence of Patrick,

Rejoice, a nostalgic communing with her beloved brother,

Celebrate, today's knowing of a simpatico connection with Dillon...

Oh, my precious and strong warriorette images,

Able to ride my gentle Friesian mare again,

Sandra believed in her rise, alive to a spirit of renewals...

Good Luck Signs

Time to rise and shine. Yes, I am alive!

Sandra was reflecting in the newest sound bites. She munched on a breakfast, truly appreciating her quintessential abundance.

Able to eat again. Healthy food. My undeniable appetite. Fifteen months of my shaky remission. And, now—my ultimate riches of this morning.

Sandra reminisced about those warriorette images within her frail body. All these months, she visualized riding with these strong warriorettes. Sandra galloped alongside them on a golden-chestnut horse, her stunning Friesian mare.

Sandra talked aloud while she dressed, speaking to a voice memo on the cell phone. Her journal stories were transcribed in the evening.

"I am bundled with soft layers, my favorite beret covering my emerging, copper-red curls, and a matching scarf to cover my *royal highness* nose and *rapturous* lips," she expressed fondly. Sandra did a u-turn, walking backward to wink into a gilded, gold mirror in her bedroom.

"Looking mighty fine, sweet woman, if I do say so," Sandra proclaimed, twirling and gliding towards a taller mirror in the entry foyer. Sandra stopped purposefully. "Check out my stylin' patchwork jeans, a fitted Italian leather jacket, and my lavender suede boots," she touted aloud, performing a grand finale swirl.

Grabbing her cell phone and a Euro pouch, Sandra went out the door, celebrating that she was also driving again. She had parallel parked her truck magnificently.

Sandra's pick-up truck had a unique granny-gear shifter, a short bed, and a step-side design. The first namesake was Bubba, declared by her faculty who were also celebrating Sandra's remission. Of course, Sandra renamed her classy and sporty pick-up. Bubbette!

The next week, the beloved colleagues tacked up a newspaper clipping on her office door, highlighting the novel popularity of pick-ups with women. They wrote boldly in red crayola: Especially for Dr. Sandra in her sporty Bubbette!

Her half-time teaching meant that Sandra would heal. She knew to partake of the daily walkabouts, a healthy diet, and savor her attitude to regain a feisty spirit.

"Today, I am turning on my voice memo again. I am parked near my favorite pathway, following a bubbling stream. Ready for a longer walkabout. Love to see my cloud images with definitive signs, the sky art, beautiful butterflies, and my animal friends," Sandra proclaimed, as she picked up the pace and kept talking aloud.

"My friends and even the colleagues agree that I am the animal whisperer wherever I am strolling," Sandra recalled giggling. "Well, Mother Earth's animals, the melodic birds, my amazing butterflies like the petticoat beauty, and the colorful dragon flies seem to appreciate my voice and the loving messages," she affirmed.

Sandra came to a halt intentionally. It was another mindful nudge. She did not take for granted her latest stamina boosts and a heightened wellness on each day.

Sandra was ecstatic to be able to sit longer on her cozy patio. She decided to eat dinner in the company of a stunning sunset. Not one, but two of her animal totem friends arrived.

"Why, hello! You are truly a sighting, my exquisite lavender-gray and double-winged dragon fly. Welcome! C'mon and join me for dinner," Sandra encouraged, in a merry voice. "Yes, I see you cocking your tiny head to listen. Thank you!"

As Sandra reached for her lemon water, this befriending dragon fly took flight. Within a minute, a red-burgundy dragon fly appeared on her chair in the same spot.

"Oh my, you are another beauty! Amazing color and a bit bigger, but double-winged as well. Now my friend, here comes a forewarning. I am reaching very carefully for my lemon water. Whoops, there you go. What is happening?"

There was a reason for Sandra's reaction. Her left arm was resting on the chair. Her relaxed hand was open. The red-burgundy beauty did not disappear. The dragon fly flew right onto her hand, tickling two fingers, and startled her. In that exact moment, the red-burgundy dragon fly soared up, up, and away. Sandra looked afar, then spoke excitedly.

"Wow, still around before you soared upward, my sweet dragon fly! I was startled, but adored the tickling sensations. Two dragon flies—my honored animal friends of my upper-north totem— represented the good luck signs of my amazing day." Sandra smiled.

"Yesterday, my good luck sign was a morpho owl butterfly, another honored, animal-totem friend. Actually, it was my revered sign, this time about the capacity of transformation. I like these daily, loving affirmations that contribute to my remission," Sandra murmured.

Sandra felt that wherever the two dragon flies flew, they sensed an unconditional caring and her conversations of genuine gratitude. Sandra continued to eat slowly, enjoying a last moment of today's spectacular hues in the skyline.

It was at sunset when Sandra's good luck signs appeared and reappeared. Two dragon flies made her heart soar with a commanding, impressive spirit. Indeed, she was transforming each day. She was an amazing survivor.

"Alas, my good luck charmers! And, what about the standout and superlative appearances and those surprise tickles?" Sandra paused, only for a few seconds.

"My gift of remission is priceless. The other gifts of today? My dragon flies and our mutual rejoicing, perhaps sealed with that loving, tickle-kiss?"

Years ago, Zion canyon park brought forth Sandra's animal totem,

Today, after the walkabouts, her patio gifted the good luck charmers,

Mutual rejoicing, a return of Sandra's commanding remission...

Orbs of Light

Look up, Francesco Ricci…
Radiant prisms of light
Look down, Francesco Ricci…

Bubbles floating across the sand, circular and festive
Become orbs of light, floating prisms like the crystal butterflies
Birthday gifts for the joys, the laughter, and your treasure-trove of dreams

Look up, Francesco Ricci…
Changes are happening
Look down, Francesco Ricci…

Bubbles floating across native waters, natural and free
Become the companionate bubbles, spiraling down a golden-hue shoreline
Birthday gifts for the joys, the laughter, and your treasure-trove of dreams

Francesco bowed his head, grateful that he was still alive for this birthday. He survived the hit-and-run accident in his sister's car.

Last year in the hospital, Paolina managed to compose "Orbs of Light" for his special day. The next day, his beloved sister graced his hand and smiled peacefully at Francesco. Then Paolina joined Papa and Mama.

This year arrived with another Paolina gift. Francesco was able to walk that golden-hue shoreline, letting the water ripples immerse his bronzed feet.

Francesco murmured Paolina's prose effortlessly. Happy tears welled in his eyes, until they rolled down each cheek.

He waded into the pristine waters, looking up and looking down at the radiant prisms of light. Immersion. Gratitude. Daydreams.

Francesco's daydreams became a journal that his soul was writing. Today arrived with this birthday gift beyond measure.

One vortex and another swirling out of reach,

Without fears, Francesco began a different immersion,

Let his soul write this next journey of moving forward...

Voices of Our Neighbors

"Are you still terrified?" I asked gingerly, watching her face very closely.

Jasmyn never hedged. "Yes! Sometimes, I pretend that I am not in my apartment. If he is at the door, I am quiet, still…" Her voice trailed off, almost a whisper. Then Jasmyn stared off into space, her eyes revealing an anxiety and the angst.

"He *always* calls when I am at work."

"Oh my, Jasmyn. What do you say?"

"I tell him that I cannot talk now and hang up."

"Have you told your boss that Denny calls at work? Your boss is so supportive, Jasmyn. Tell him today, so that your phone extension is changed and all your calls are recorded," I urged, knowing that my caring tone with a brief pause always helped Jasmyn.

"Your boss has made sure that you travel out of town on business to get away for your well-being and safety. He has the security personnel walk you to a parking garage and your car. Hey, no secrecy with your boss or me, Jasmyn."

"You are right. I have business calls to make, but I shall talk again on my lunch break. I promise—no secrets."

A few hours later, my dear friend divulged her next secrets. My teachings in social work at the local community college and certain women in my classes came full circle with Jasmyn's naked truths.

I taught about the domestic violence, the yearly abuses, the horrific secrets, and the false promises. Like Jasmyn, certain women decided to divulge their horrors. I secured the reputable shelters and their safe havens, but the secrecy re-entered my thoughts immediately.

Secrecy of abuse… Imagine twenty people every minute. Overall, 86 percent of the abuse victims are reported as a girlfriend or a boyfriend. The physical abuse for women is one in four and one in seven men, when the abuse is by an intimate partner.

The Department of Justice reports that 84 percent of women experience spousal abuse. Their marriages often continue without the counseling or any improvements. Promises to change become the unfulfilled wishes.

The battering does not disappear magically, but lingers as the undocumented domestic violence. Jasmyn owned too many of these truths.

During the year that I moved into the neighborhood, Jasmyn became my witty, endearing friend. I heard about the first burdens that I had already come to suspect. I recalled Jasmyn's words, almost like yesterday.

"Denny lies and goes out on me. He tries to possess me, but I keep trying to change things. I try to cope. He leaves with no word on his whereabouts. Suddenly, Denny will reappear," Jasmyn said, confessing to his adultery. But, there was something else that underscored a daily terror.

When her real secrecy—domestic violence—was relinquished, I confirmed my suspicions. I did not know for sure. Victims often remain silent, too anxious. Unfortunately, the societal judgements are still rendered in their neighborhoods or at work. Jasmyn was no different.

One day, Jasmyn was gone. I stopped by and called for days, but still no answers. My stomach was doing outrageous flip-flops. I finally reached her at work.

"Are you okay, Jasmyn?" My words tumbled out.

Jasmyn answered in a cool, professional tone. "Yes." Silence. Then she recognized my voice and let go, a warm tone and talks that significant friends hold dear. Jasmyn had been trying to reach me.

That day I learned about the ugly traumas. In a barely audible, tense voice Jasmyn's recent secrets escaped.

"Last week, I ran away. Snuck outside. I ran to the nearest hiding spot, an abandoned barn down the street in a meadow. A restless sleep. My only companions—paralyzing fears and the physical pains—from Denny's battering of my breasts and my stomach. My mind played the games with me. Go back, *never* go back," Jasmyn managed to share breathlessly.

I spoke quickly from my aching heart. "I am here for you, Jasmyn. *Love* you!"

Jasmyn replied softly, "I know. *Love* you, Angelica."

Jasmyn left for good. But today, her phone time at work was limited. Days later, we met in another town, making sure that it was a crowded restaurant. I knew that I would ask again for a long time.

"Are you still terrified?"

"Always!" Her tone was adamant, but Jasmyn was finally willing to take control of a distressed and traumatic life as much as possible. I remember Jasmyn's half-smile and lovely hugs that day in our Mediterranean Blue Grotto Bistro.

"I feel blessed with *real* friends. You are so special Angelica, but I shall never stay with you. It is too close. Denny would return to the neighborhood, especially to your home, and try to find me."

"Let him show up at my home! Listen carefully, my dear Jasmyn. I am finding you a reputable shelter—your safe haven pronto. I shall help with the protective court orders and locate a security apartment near your work site, Jasmyn!"

"You are my amazing grace..." Jasmyn's voice got softer. "Angelica, your short namesake is Angel. You are my *earth Angel!"* We hugged and swayed together, much like the rocking-comfort cuddles for a distressed child.

After her safe return to work, I continued to drive a few miles to teach two classes. Later that week, Jasmyn's husband did stop by to visit me, attempting to mask his transparent motives. Denny still believed that nobody in the neighborhood knew their secrets. He kept repeating the dark messages to Jasmyn in no uncertain terms, before her runaway escape and the final departure.

Incredible! Even my young dog, a lovable German Shepard to everyone, shied away from Denny that unforgettable day and started to growl. Denny's face got red, as he tried to laugh off the obvious incident.

My thoughts were roaming all over the map that evening.

Jasmyn needs a safe haven for sure. Denny is the real deal, not to be taken lightly. I am calling Jasmyn tomorrow about the reputable shelter. I did find an opening that same afternoon.

I know in my heart, dear Jasmyn is ready to move. She even talks about her company Employee Assistance Program as another vital lifeline.

Jasmyn's counselor is also emphatic. "You should be in the company of a friend at all times."

Jasmyn and I would find out exactly what that foreshadowing meant.

Weeks passed. My repetitive question of compassion was never bypassed.

"Are you ok?" Jasmyn knew what I meant.

"For now, Angelica. It is like a show. Denny is stalking me all the time—my *every* move."

"What about the court order?" I asked, somehow managing to keep my composure.

"Denny is evasive—not at home and changing his jobs. The police will not and cannot do a thing without the order. Angelica, I have to be set up before I call."

Even my professional insights did not alter certain episodes. There were seconds when I would literally forget to breathe, especially when Jasmyn conveyed a scenario with her shudders.

"It is a living hell. Will I have to do this forever, until the end of time? When I am on my *deathbed*, then will the police try to help me, Angelica?"

"Oh my God, Jasmyn!" We hugged for an eternity.

Neither of us gave up. Our visits, the daily calls, our dialogues about her counseling and work, the church, and a friend who lived next door became Jasmyn's divine lifelines.

"How ironical or meant to be? My *male* boss always empathizes and tries to restrict my calls. He arranges my flights and the necessary reprieves to our California company."

"I am so proud and beyond grateful with each and every one of your proactive actions, my dearest friend!"

The court order was finally a done deal. It was the legal restraint, but not a guarantee of a foolproof protection. There was a courageous rite of passage. Jasmyn's bottom line, after the rollercoaster horrors and the years of silence that imprisoned her soul, was the epitome of a profound courage.

"The before is a greater fear for me...than the now."

"Our candid dialogues and trust, your courage, an empathic boss and counselor, and moving forward are beginning to solidify your new reality checks. Once upon a time, there was only a dim light, even with the counseling attempts. Denny gave up immediately. Now, your present world has changed forever, Jasmyn!" I expressed, with elated tears and a lingering embrace.

There were still terrifying moments. I was swayed and horrified with the relentless and unpredictable incidents that Jasmyn shared—too matter of fact.

"He got past security. His facade or a pay off. In my apartment parking lot, Denny pulled out a hand gun, just to show me. My son was furious, wanting to threaten him. With my coaxing, my son held back. He felt quite helpless. Now, my son has become so protective of my whereabouts. We always hung tough and together. A lot of love!"

I stretched to do everything I knew and taught, always listening to my heart and staying mindful. Jasmyn was stronger as the months progressed, like what she did when Denny pulled the gun in a vacant area of her apartment parking lot.

"I confronted him. I know when I can do that," Jasmyn pronounced flatly.

"God, how did you know that Denny would not shoot you?" My words tumbled out. Goose bumps were already creeping over my body from the envisioned what-ifs.

"I know when I can confront. And when I can't," Jasmyn added, without any pause.

Jasmyn broke her toxic patterns when she filed and obtained a divorce. During the whole process, Denny tried to antagonize, manipulate, and use her religion as grounds for not divorcing.

Jasmyn had pressed onward against the odds. Now, she spoke candidly about the past. "Denny was never religious, but that did not matter. Angelica, you sensed a false pretense and Denny's manipulations, even when you first moved into our neighborhood."

"I *really* did, Jasmyn. There were intuitive feelings of something very dark, an undercurrent of a horrendous pain happening in your relationship. I recall one day after your return from church, I sensed Denny's facade of joking etched with a sarcasm and a smug smile. Shortly after, I stared at his face. Denny's eyes were dark and his expression had changed. I did not care what Denny thought. It was your glance at me in those minutes that nailed my intuitive feelings of a much darker abyss, my endearing friend."

"Yes! I felt strongly that you suspected something was not right. I noticed that you did not miss any subtle or the transparent minutes. Angelica, I am *so blessed* that you moved into our neighborhood."

During the tougher trials and Denny's intimidations, Jasmyn's counselor reinforced how to go forward with the transition periods at work and her daily living. She confirmed that her friends who elected to stay, the divorce, a legal restraint, and the supportive employers were the healthy dynamics in Jasmyn's healing process.

Jasmyn valued who was in her corner. She spoke calmly about this higher road.

"My empathic male boss provides opportunities for training at other job sites. My weekend job enhances my monetary situation. My strong religious belief provides a temple of peacefulness."

"Those truths are beautiful and your benevolent gifts, Jasmyn!"

"Absolutely! They are priceless. Plus, my strong-willed son who endured the earlier, intermittent beatings keeps my unlisted phone number and my new security residence our secret."

It was later in Jasmyn's journey, but her ex-husband had a live-in girlfriend. His calls at her work site diminished. These transitions in Denny's life were lifelines, both real and visionary for Jasmyn.

"I shall live in a security complex until Denny is no longer around. That will be forever. But, I am more determined than ever, Angelica."

"I know! Jasmyn, I cherish and recognize your new determination and the different directions—for your son and your special self-care. You *deserve* the best, my courageous and precious friend!"

The next weeks of teaching were more powerful than ever. I affirmed my related teachings would remain vivid, the lifetime lessons and reciprocal learning for all of us. Indeed, my teachings became the mindful echoes in my heart and daily thoughts.

Are we attending to the voices of acquaintances, our neighbors, our friends, or even the strangers whose paths cross our lifetime journey? Rural, suburban, and urban. Young, middle-age, and even the elderly. Wealthy, middle class, and the impoverished. The yearly statistics—data reports and the projections—were the invisible witnesses of the locales, the diverse ages, and every economic level.

Maybe, we suspect. Perhaps, we are hesitant on where to begin, what is intrusive, or a multitude of what-ifs enter our mind. The signs of physical abuse are often hidden, even with the summer outfits. So are any emotional upheavals and the prevalent psychological scars.

Across the years, Jasmyn endured the unconscionable acts of physical abuse and the psychological scars. Nowadays, there were courageous promises and Jasmyn's new convictions.

I was visiting her at another neighborhood gathering. Jasmyn and I laughed heartily, then giggled softly. Our eyes meant in a spiritual way that made our heartspeake come naturally.

"You radiate joy—an outer and the inner beauty. How happy you are, Jasmyn!"

Jasmyn smiled readily. "I am feeling *much* better." She laughed again. "Jasmyn is getting her act together, Angelica!"

Earlier, I overheard Jasmyn talking to an acquaintance. "I love my life now."

I looked at their nearby chairs. The woman was nodding, as if she knew Jasmyn's story.

Few people realized that Jasmyn had taken the high road. It was still a pathway less traveled by women in our more open and compassionate society.

A familiar warmth and an extraordinary peacefulness swelled up in my heart. I believed that one woman counted.

Jasmyn deserved the respect, an evolving self-love, her zigzag paths to a stellar happiness, and her new evolution. Jasmyn's son and daughter-in-law were also doing fine.

"I shall be a happy mi-ma soon," Jasmyn pronounced ecstatically, while we were at that neighborhood gathering.

"Superlative, Jasmyn. Crazy-happy for you! Your son and daughter in-law as well." We bear-hugged, always for an eternity. My thoughts were floating again.

I recall thinking to myself in that very moment of our bear-hugs. Everyone owns a story with the different layers of darkness.

No more! Her lurid, murky, and pitch-black abyss was diminishing. No more!

Jasmyn is a courageous role model for the women who are still debating when, where, and how to tell-all. Jasmyn never forgets the darkness…

"When another woman hears my story and gets all fired up, she can feel the chills. She will know. I see people at work that live each day with a bad attitude. So I told myself I had to change and started. I still do certain things. I keep candid literature on abused women and the self-help books beside my bed. I read and reread. It is so plain." Jasmyn paused for a few seconds.

My rereading reminds me, just like yesterday." Jasmyn's voice trailed off, almost a murmur. Then a bolder and commanding voice proclaimed today's truths.

"There are no guarantees, no quick fixes, or a scheduled day for enlightenment, Angelica. At a job, at individual churches, in different communities, or our neighborhoods, none of us can predict the exact timing. You, my sister-friend Angelica, accepted my outstretched hand and offered me the next lifelines. Those priceless moments, worth a queen's ransom, just arrived at the perfect time."

I continued my teachings, especially the uplifting inspirations of Jasmyn's strong attributes and other women's truth-seeking. I offered my insights and proactive actions regarding the safe havens.

"Each of us makes a choice to become our sister's or brother's keeper," I emphasized. That consistent remark caused my students to speak up, especially after I connected our readings and my commitments to help.

"Our class readings support the developmental counselors, the psychologists, the valued educators, and other professionals who report the horrific abuses. They become involved as caring professionals, the concerned citizens, or the treasured friends." I paused, glancing at the faces in my entire class.

"We take the bold, courageous risks whenever we dare, right? We say things like, 'Are you okay? Let's talk about who can help.' Yes, Cheryl? Share your beliefs."

"Yes! That reminds these brave women of a warm feeling of community, a genuine helping, and the truth that we intend to pursue matters. It is that elusive process of changing our lives, too. Opening these doors signals a real commitment and our sense of shared responsibility."

"Spot on, Cheryl. So perceptive! Since infancy, like an enormous sponge, we venture along in life, soaking up our lifetime experiences. Before long, we evolve with the personalized life scripts. Go ahead, Amy."

"Certain situations boomerang though, leaving us hurt. With these abused women, they own such *horrific* physical and deeper emotional scars."

"Perceptive and real truths! All understatements, Cheryl and Amy. Each of us inevitably learns from our deepest struggles, as affirmed by an early developmentalist like Erikson. Unlike the perfect Pollyanna stories, several of us want to strive during the peaks and valleys in life. We yearn to find our inner homeostasis, much like Jean Piaget's writings. You know, that balance in our daily living. And, likewise with our surprises—the unexpected or an unsettling event."

"And what about those trust versus distrust cycles?" blurted out Juanita, always bold with her authentic compassion.

"Ah, your empathic question… To expand on Juanita's compassion, let me underscore a few confessionals, like it or not. Trust and distrust will come to our doorsteps for a lifetime. But, it is *how* each of us copes. Each of us makes our unique accommodations. Remember? In hindsight, I truly learned from my tougher times. Our courageous confessions?"

Ron raised his hand, but then just spoke. "Most of us admit, often after those adjustments, that we *really* learned from our tougher or the toughest times. I know. I have confessed several truths to my *best* friend."

"Absolutely, Ron! Being present, like your *best* friend, often helps us through the toughest adjustments. It is a choice, right?"

"Yahhh. Being there for another person, a dear friend of mine during his tougher times, meant that we can and do reach out. I hope that I began to empower him during his difficult times and remain a powerful, can-do role model. I had also experienced horrific traumas and a similar abuse as well," affirmed Rosa.

"Thank you for your choice, Rosa! Being there to boost his self esteem was a real commitment. Each of us can reaffirm the positive connections between our self-esteem and those lasting achievements, especially when our efforts and the support make the 'never say never' diminish in someone's life."

"And what about the patterns that evolve?" probed Ron.

"True. So true, Ron. Our class readings reveal that the pattern remains transgenerational. Violence begets violence. Secrecy and keeping things in the closet, right? Breaking the cycle is not an easy step, but the shelters, the different hotlines, the community counselors, and people like us who are a supportive friend make a tougher change seem possible. Beginning to rewrite your life script takes tremendous courage. That courage begins a new shaping, another pattern that entices the self-worth. Hey, all of us want to get rid of enormous hurts and invisible scars, eh?"

The classroom buzzed with commentaries. "Right, Dr. Angelica!" "Totally!" "Commitment and our self-promises to change. Choices and options." "You taught us so much, Dr. Angelica! You live your commitments. A beacon of light for all of us who are lucky to be in your classes."

"My radiant light goes out to each of you. Our class time is over, but I want to reinforce an ultimate hope—ALL of your attitudes and the authentic actions completed in the challenging internships? I *celebrate* each of you!" Dr. Angelica added, as she scanned their earnest faces.

She raised her arm, pointing one finger upward to an imagined sky. Everyone stayed in that defining moment, listening to her closure.

"At work, at play, in a neighborhood, or with cherished, significant others—we rarely predict an exact timing to extend our hand. These moments for becoming our sister's or brother's keeper just arrive. Even nature risks saying spring too soon."

Even nature risks saying spring too soon,

Befriending and extending a hand to be our sister's or brother's keeper,

Angelica's outreach, the lifelines, and Jasmyn's life balance mattered...

Revolution-Evolution

"Seeing is beyond a realm of sight. Be attentive to today's and tomorrow's imagery. Witness your inheritance," invoked Troy. "Look to all of the sacred corners of our earth."

"The power of intention comes in any second or a minute during our journey. No hesitation. Entrust that a special time and the space are forthcoming to manifest your life balance and a new legacy," added Sabrina.

"Each of us covets the new endings, especially when we learn and expand with the mystic spaces. There are such resonant messages," affirmed Wayne, nodding his approval to Sabrina.

"I have found an intimate place of breath called—my calm, my solace, and my assurance. My lifetime journey is quite different now," explained Amelia.

"I believe and I entrust. There is a time for unveiling our truths, but what a loving-kindness when we listen to the voices of everyone!" added Justin.

"I keep learning to soar. My lucid dreaming and the daydreaming are part of my core being and becoming," Hortense acknowledged, with a slow and deliberate voice.

"Homeless, floating like an empty balloon over the tall majesty of the pines? Never. There are no castaways!" exclaimed Trinity.

"The synapses and neurons of my amazing heart inform my brain," Cheri murmured. "I sense the vapors of a divine presence."

"Our attentive and attending spirit is always ready to evolve," declared Thanos. "Receive and accept."

"Pause for a few minutes throughout the day or eve. Ease into your inhale-exhale breaths. Let your mantra become the martyrs of sound. Greet what it means to become a visionary," intoned Lakota.

Each week the group sat in a meditative circle. They reached out to clasp another member's hand, as they shared. At the end of their gift-giving to one another, the group paused to take three, deeper breaths. They meditated in the silence for a half-hour.

A special closure followed the meditation. Everyone repeated their group mantra, while listening to Lakota's gentle drumming. Their voices in this chant created a special haven, the gifted circle of light, and a heartfelt echo with Lakota's drumming.

"Revolution-Evolution."

Optimism is a happiness magnet. If you stay positive, good things and good people will be drawn to you.

Time for unveiling their heartfelt echoes of truths and a lucid daydreaming,

Martyrs of sound enfold their drumming circle and their attunement to humanity,

Cheri, Thanos, Lakota, and their circle of friends seek a luminous road, honoring the unknown...

Potential budding and blossoming on Dr. Royce's journey compel her utmost attention,

She gathers this abundance, like a cornucopia of sustenance,

Smell the roses, soar higher, and seek the offbeat pathway...

Intersections and Passages

The semester had just started. She went by my office four times, finally decided to stop.

I commanded my brain to engage. *Which class? Blast, what is her name?*

"Hi, Esmeralda," I said in a split-second, with a smile and my hand gesture, an invitation to sit down. Suddenly, I remembered our motivation class. I astonished myself when her name popped back so quickly.

Hesitant steps, but Esmeralda entered my eclectic office. She stared momentarily at my best friend's oil painting of a majestic, snowcapped mountain in the company of a soothing skyline. A disappearing path, trailing along the swift stream, looked like it overflowed right into my office. My friend's artistry was breathtaking and a treasured keepsake.

I had returned two weeks ago to this unique university, after beginning last fall semester as a well-liked and talented Assistant Professor. Even with the prestigious accolades, all of us were affectionately called the "green or newbie profs."

I watched and waited. Esmeralda sat down slowly, clasping her hands tightly. She kept the downcast eyes, until I spoke after my inner reflections.

If only my favorite chair could embrace Esmeralda, as it had my former students who remained in touch. Interrupting my own musing, I manage to initiate a simple conversation.

"Esmeralda, it is nice that that you would stop by my office. What might I do for you?"

She looked up slowly to scan my face for the first time and smiled hesitantly. "I wanted to talk to you about my class participation. I really liked your motivation class, looked forward to it…" Her meek voice trailed off.

With downcast eyes again, Esmeralda shared a tip of her iceberg. "But, I was preoccupied. I just wanted you to know I was trying to concentrate better." She began biting her bottom lip.

I had learned one thing about my office hours. There were days when you had nanoseconds before another meeting or a class. It would not be the first time the beginning of an important dialogue ended abruptly.

"Esmeralda, nontraditional-age students like yourself are usually taking two or three courses, have a husband and children, or are single parents working a part time job. Sometimes, it takes a few semesters to adjust the priorities, juggle all the needs, and concentrate more effectively." Esmeralda stared at my oak floor, then looked up longingly.

"I have another class now, but please free to stop and talk again, Esmeralda." As I rose from my leather chair, gathering my colorful tote from Chile, I could not pinpoint my concern.

Our eyes met. Esmeralda smiled back hesitantly, before making a beeline for my door. I headed swiftly up two flights of stairs and into the bustling hallway to my leadership class.

On the way there, I waved to other students and my Chair of the department. When the seasoned and still-green-around-the-gills faculty gathered for advising and earlier meetings, Dr. Swan made it clear.

"Just Fred is appropriate and preferred," he announced. "Save the Dr. Fred Swan for the upper crust across the street," he joked.

I headed down the sardine-packed hallway to my classroom. "Don't forget the committee meeting about our wannabe graduate students," Fred reminded, in a singsong voice with a grin. He was a humorous, an involved leader with his personal reminders. Fred sent witty, informative emails or left quick updates on our voice mails.

"Not a chance!" I teased, pretending to sound threatening. Our laughter reverberated in the less crowded hallway. I scurried into the doorway of my class, plunking down my Chilean tote.

This year, most of our classrooms had the modernized furniture and several redesigned spaces for the new technological devices. Greeting students coming into class, I simultaneously reflected about my Chair.

Fred appears to be knowledgeable, even-keel, supportive, and humorous. He is politically savvy about the drama of university life.

At least Fred acknowledges the brand new and still-green professors. Yes, Dr. Royce, you are the latter. I smirk to myself. I suspect, like my former university, the new blood in the department polarizes a few colleagues. Time reveals all...

Hi, Dr. R!" crooned Jim with his easy smile, causing me to shift my attention to the present moment.

"How goes it?" he quizzed. Jim appeared to be a student who gave new professors a fair chance to prove themselves.

"Not bad. Makes me wonder what's going to go astray!" I bantered.

"Yup, I know that feeling, Dr. R." Then he grinned like a Cheshire cat.

Some students were shocked by his informality. Like Fred, I was comfortable with my earned doctorate, but my students had been invited to use my range of namesakes, if they were comfortable. They knew the proper times to address professors in an expected, professional manner.

I started our class. "Our journeys begin with a *first* step. So, let's stretch that funky gray matter in our brains, especially at 8:00 a.m. and give Monday a grandiose kick-start." Groans and laughter circulated around the room, enticing their wake-up calls.

"I want you to think of leadership examples from the growing years," I added. "Childhood and adolescence. Dah… Remember?" I probed with twinkling eyes and a wink. "Ah, my classroom is about to percolate!"

"Dr. Royce, I was an officer in a youth fellowship for three years. By popular demand, I guess," offered Tina, with her usual humble touch.

"Magnificent! A leader who was sought after. Voila!" Then I reinforced our class readings. "Those years contributed to your preparation, even success in future leadership roles." Now was the right moment.

"Who knows? In one or two years after graduation, each of you in this room could be the CEO of your own company. You could become a chair on a prestigious, meaningful board. Even donate time for your leadership of a nonprofit or volunteer organization," I offered, with a sincere vision of their potential journeys in today's world.

"Dr. R., I was co-captain of my peewee team," Jim interjected, as he stood up. Then he entertained everyone with his eloquent bows to the four corners of the classroom.

His peers were primed. "Wow, what a man, Jim!" teased Naomi. "You go, my brother!" interjected Juan. Shawn and his groupies applauded with arms held high over their heads, especially when Jim bowed to their corner.

The focus came back to me. The students were not quite sure of my quirky responses this early in the semester.

"Yay, Jim was a legend at five years old! Imagine that." I laughed heartily with an encouraging, thumbs-up sign. I jumped at the opportunity to intertwine the related research findings.

"Now, I want all of you to be encouraging and the praiseworthy judges as to what traits Tina and Jim owned as true-blue leaders, especially at very early stages of development. All of you recall—that swelling pride in the real experiences."

The class was on a roll. "Sterling character that was admired by peers." "A willingness to listen." "Definitely a shared decision-making with the team spirit." "Able to display a sense of humor and flexible with diverse personalities." Each student was on target. They were psyched, especially as we changed to a virtual reality game with a paired learner and the random rotations.

I left my leadership class on a natural high. The buzz of students' intrinsic desires was what genuine teachers wanted to witness. I held high hopes and steadfast beliefs that my classes and our reciprocal learning would continue to spark an inspiring, memorable semester. Little did I know.

I grabbed a quick lunch at the student union. That meeting time to discuss our wannabe graduate students was approaching. My mind strayed back to Fred. I ate my vegetarian soup, a wheat bagel, drank spring water, and scrawled notes for our meeting. My thoughts floated to the other day.

His secretary makes an obvious point to share that Fred is divorced. Hmm, I am daydreaming or wondering. Is he divorced for a few years? I do not have a clue. But, I am curious when other professors and the secretaries ask how his Melinda is getting along in elementary school. Back to my priority list for our faculty meeting.

Man, I could write volumes. It was more like a book on how to survive grad school—for our department and probably varied departments on campus. The grandiose, mediocre, bogus, distressing, uplifting, and bad-to-the-bone experiences were often shared behind closed doors at universities, our national conferences, or the unsuspected places. Indeed, the parking lots were the best venue.

On my way across campus, I caught a glimpse of a different Esmeralda with two friends. Overindulgence in my splendid intuition? I caught her gaze at the elevator in our building, waved, and smiled. Esmeralda smiled, that hesitant smile.

I refrained from saying, "Stop by again." I still could not shake my concern.

It was a superb faculty meeting. Agenda followed and completed, relevant questions, and more innovative ideas. "Any last thoughts?" Fred inquired. He scanned the faculty room with our comfortable chairs, comfy couches, and matching pillows. I overheard they were actually allowed in our budget requests.

"C'mon, both seasoned and green profs, strut your stuff," Fred encouraged. He seemed to enjoy reviving any last tidbits after a completed agenda.

I checked my scrawled notes and fancy doodling. "How about an informal get-together with simulations of real happenings for our wannabe graduate students? Why not at the laid-back lounge of the university club where the munchies won't make them croak?" I added, in my undaunted manner. Everyone seemed quite attentive, not ready to charge off to their next adventure.

"Send playful invitations to all faculty and seasoned grad students to make our wannabe grad students feel like a part of our program sooner rather than later in their pathfinding," I elaborated, with a jovial spirit. "They will meet us soon enough in our courses. We could save face now!"

Colleagues like Wendy added to the entertainment and provided a sincere support. Laughter and applause followed when Fred winked to the seasoned professors.

"Magnificent. All heads are nodding. So, how about it, Dr. Royce? Want to be the chair of your first department committee?" He watched my face and the panicked expressions.

"Hey, do not have a stroke yet. There will be infamous committee members to offer their help," Fred added. "Right, volunteers?" he emphasized, twinkling at my colleagues. There were several chuckles and an actual volunteer or two.

"Sure!" I bantered, revealing my Dr. R. confident air. My brain and heart were also clicking and pounding rhythmically—testing time for the still-green professor. "Not to worry," as my Brit friend Whitney said to everything. This time, our classes or other adventures met our quick departures.

"Wendy, I appreciate your fun-loving ideas and collegial support," I remarked, as we left for our office appointments.

"Hey, we need the NEW blood! The old geysers rarely suggest the fun-loving, high jinks, or any different approaches. In neutral gear, I swear. Just coasting, until whenever or their summers off in Europe."

Wendy and I improvised for the gaiety and a memorable welcome for our wannabe grads, before she departed for an evening class. Fred and I were the last ones to leave. "Welcome to academe. Strut your stuff, do your best job. I guarantee that Dr. R. will be chair of not only this department committee, but also a *biggie* university committee soon."

He lingered longer, as if in a trance. "Brings back my colorful memories."

I stood there for a few minutes. I guess Fred sensed his trance.

"You have got time to spread your wings and soar. Do not start worrying about things that have not happened." He quickly turned his tan arm to check his watch. "Gottta go. Melinda."

"Bye, Dr. Fred. Thanks, I think!" He turned on his way out the door and grinned.

I had mixed feelings. Fred obviously stuck me as chair, yet he was encouraging. Well, no fretting, as he noted. "Just go for it, Dr. Royce," I replied out loud, spurring my determination.

I was truly enthused with the possibilities and flashed back to my early morning class. Well, here I was questioning Dr. R's newest leadership role. I thought about what Jim might say.

"Some role model, Dr. R." I laughed at and with myself, as I left the empty room.

I hustled to my office, grabbed a stack of papers on my beautiful oak desk for grading, and locked my door. Home was near the university. On the way, I was reflecting in sound bites.

Great leftover meal. Time to grade. Oops, the absent-minded prof syndrome. Forgot the other papers on my shelf. Time for a U-turn, Baby Azul! I am just scooting back to the university.

I grabbed another stack of papers in the deep tray on my book shelf, locked my door, and remembered that I had also forgotten to check my mailbox.

I perused quickly. As I turned to leave, Fred appeared from nowhere. I jumped and emitted a weird noise.

"Sorry, did not mean to scare you," Fred said, with a hint of a grin, given my weird noise, I suppose. Shortly thereafter, a girl about eight years old bounded into the mailroom. Blonde hair, hazel eyes, and a full grin. I began to wonder.

This joyful cherub is Melinda. Fred's hair is dark brown, a few auburn highlights. I wonder about his former wife, but I am interrupted.

"Such dedication to the job, huh? Just had to return?" Melinda stood there with a bigger grin, precious dimples, and twinkling hazel eyes. Of course, she was taking in the scene.

"No, the absent-minded prof syndrome snagged me," I admitted, with an entertaining giggle. I waved the papers in my hand and made sure to stuff them into my colorful, Chilean tote.

Melinda and Fred had play time, as we walked to the parking lot. She held Fred's swinging hand. When we stopped to say goodbyes, she gave me a hug and planted a smooch on my cheek.

"Why, thank you, joyful spirit!" as I tapped her nose three times and laughed. "Take care. Have your Dad read a super bedtime story!"

"I always do, Dr. R.," Fred responded in a playful tone. My muses wanted to interrupt that evening.

Back at the ranch, I let my muses enter and exit in between the grading of my papers. My students are blossoming at the beginning of fall semester. Spring semester is going to be top notch. My new summer course is already closed. Yawning, I know it is past my usual beddie-bye time.

I was meandering out of the mailroom with my alma mater mug filled to the brim with freshly brewed coffee. I noticed Esmeralda down the hallway, a few doors from my office. She still had not spoken very much in my spring class.

I shouted. "Esmeralda!" She turned, obviously startled.

"Sorry for my booming voice. I just thought you might be looking for me. I was in the mailroom. I wanted to catch you." I sensed Esmeralda was considering a departure.

"How about a cup of brew with me?"

"No thanks," Esmeralda replied, avoiding my eyes.

I teased. "How about a plain ole' visit?" I enticed, but waited.

Finally, she looked at me and replied in a low, barely audible tone, "Okay."

Esmeralda was still uncomfortable in my favorite chair, but seemed to relax today with my nonintrusive questions about her credit hours and my general advising. When my phone rang, she literally jumped out of that cushy chair.

"I'll go now. You are *very* busy." Before I could gesture to wait a minute, Esmerelda bolted.

I was receiving calls from my students for advising, my new course, and keeping in touch. I had to finish my final grades before heading off to California.

As I took the stairs in lieu of the clamoring, to-be-fixed elevators, I heard the student grapevines about the courses and potential professors to take this summer. "Not bad,

Dr. R.," I surmised, while eavesdropping and moving down the multitude of steps to the main foyer.

The academic year had zoomed by for me. Wendy was a co-chair on other departmental committees, coaching and cautioning me of any deeper abyss. I was complimented by her old geysers who really liked the outcomes of my efforts. Fred continued to cajole.

"I shall put you in the limelight next time," he teased. I smiled, but still wondered. My California visit was a short reprieve before the first summer session. The pace was wicked fast, four times as fast as the regular semester. Wendy teased me about acquiring a fan club, but I knew being smug too soon was a pitfall.

Self-talk again... You do not reach every student, Dr. Royce. It is always a learning curve. My inner voice is ready to continue. Ironically, Esmeralda shows up at that moment, literally popping into my office.

This time, Esmerelda paced, refusing to sit. Then she began a much-needed monologue. I urged her to sit in my comfy, favorite chair. Instead, Esmeralda bit her lip, paused, and hunkered down into the chair.

Her grades, a lack of concentration, and a preoccupation fueled her anxiety. There was another confession. Her husband was cheating, often leaving for days. Essentially, her only daughter and she had no monies for food and the rent. Finally, Esmeralda could not stomach the realities. I gently asked her who was there for any guidance and the ongoing support.

"You. I thought you might guide me. I *knew* you would understand." I let her distressful sobs, then falling tears come forth. I reached for Esmeralda's hands. The rawness of the hurts registered in our eyes. I put my brain in high gear that eve.

My soul-filled heart is replaying our dialogues and my projections of a forward momentum. I need to make confidential calls at the university about our housing for single parents with one or two children. Then I need to call an esteemed colleague in financial aid for the forthcoming schooling costs.

Esmeralda and her daughter are going to our safe haven, a dormitory converted to apartments for single women and their child or two children. Her reprieves make a difference in the gradual, courageous changes to their life. She continues to come to classes and partake of our effective counseling center. Esmerelda visits in my favorite chair nowadays.

I did not browbeat myself for my former attempts. I trusted an intuition and my intentions now. Esmerelda and I shared updates. A divorce was finalized and paid in-full. Her ex-husband became the absent Dad and paid irregular child support.

When Esmerelda was quiet in classes, I knew the real reasons. Our helping professionals in the curve and my endeavors were making a noticeable difference in her quality of living.

The fast-paced summer session was a blur, but another keepsake arrived. I was departing in the next week for California to rejuvenate, play, and visit my family and close friends. I had a few tidbits left on my plate before my lovely San Diego journey.

His office door was ajar. Fred grinned, as I entered doing a tiptoe-maneuver with a funky smile.

"How goes it, Dr. R.?"

He must have had Jim in class. Before I could answer, Fred spoke again. "So, you think you will be here *next* year?" he quizzed.

"Yeah. Gotta check out what a 'biggie limelight' is all about…" I joked, letting my voice trail off. We were professionals, but our bantering had become part of a nice rapport.

"Hey, I shall come through. Give me time to pick 'the biggie' in the university setting," Fred threatened, with another jovial chuckle.

Both of us stopped our banter to smirk at one another.

"Now, how about the last committee report that we need to discuss before you leave for the mystical and enchanting California?" Fred double-checked his watch at the same time.

Both of us spoke melodically. "Melinda!"

Fred paused. "Well, why don't you come to my place tonight and we shall go over the report?"

Faculty members in our department had been to his home for brief visits to pick up or drop off reports during the evening. He knew other faculty and administrators at the university quite well. All of us knew that Fred would be at home with Melinda.

"Sure. Is early eve okay?" I watched his face.

"Fine. See you then." Fred had looked up from his computer. I detected a sparkle. My heart talks began on the short drive home in Baby Azul.

Face it, Dr. R. It is the end of the first summer session and you are leaving. There is that quality time for a discussion of an important report and seeing joyful Melinda. Fred is picking up Melinda ASAP, so they are probably at home in fifteen minutes.

I arrived around 7 p.m. Melinda bounded outdoors, proceeding to tell me the latest scoop.

"Daddy is talking to Mom, so we can play." She stood there, hands on her small hips with a big girl grin.

"Yo Melinda, what if I do not want to play?" I teased.

"You *always* play with me!" Melinda declared, as I found her favorite tickle spot.

"You act just like a kid," she announced, as if the idea never crossed my mind and playful heart.

"And, you *love* that," I said, tickling her again. Melinda squealed and ran around the lush grass of the front yard in bare feet. The sunlight was peeking through the fresh-scented pines and the vintage oaks. The fresh breeze felt marvelous.

Ahoy, here came Zany, their black lab. The name suited him. Melinda ran after the frisbee. They ran into each other.

She lay giggling on the ground as Zany put his gargantuan paw on her stomach, giving a slew of kisses on her tiny chin. Suddenly, Zany paused, cocked his head, and stared at me with his please-play eyes.

"Oh Zany, I do not want your slobber kisses. Stay with Melinda!" I yelled, which made Melinda giggle hysterically. Zany took my cue and lapped her bare toes. My thoughts began to roam from our playtime.

For a few minutes, I want to daydream about Fred on the phone with her mother, Trish. It is several years after their divorce. Fred is the primary parent who raises and loves Melinda from day one. Everyone affirms those truths without any reservations. Apparently, Trish calls intermittently.

Fred was a willing caretaker and a loving father. Adjustments had been made, but we heard there were still episodes. People in the department expressed a sincere empathy for Melinda and Fred.

Melinda came bounding back with Zany. Oops, while I was reflecting, I certainly missed a prized scene or two.

"Melinda, let me throw that slobber-frisbee. Go for it, Zany." He took my cue and waited for the next tricks.

"Oh yay, let's try some new tricks!"

No doubts. Melinda and I were definitely double trouble for Zany.

If we were captured on video, we deserved a blue ribbon or the golden trophy. Fred stood on a porch that encircled their two-story Tudor home.

He was witness to our klutzy moves and the dizzying falls. Melinda and I landed on the lush green grass. We laughed outrageously when Melinda began to snort.

"Melinda, you will need to settle down—just a bit," Fred joked, helping us off the ground. "Is that ever possible?" he teased, as we tried to stifle our next round of enthralling giggles.

"S-s-sure, Daddy!" She grabbed his hand, smooched it, and ran up the porch stairs. Melinda pivoted on the porch, waved, and giggled before she disappeared through the exquisite wood and bevel-glass door.

All of us shared a huge bowl of fresh popcorn before Melinda's bedtime. The spring water with fresh-squeezed lemons was perfect.

"I shall *miss* you, Dr. Royce," Melinda confessed, skipping to give me a hug and her Zany-style kiss. Then came an earnest face as she stared into my twinkling eyes. "You are my *favorite* professor in the department. No…in the *whole* university!"

I shall miss you, too. Thanks for the rave reviews in the department, love. I bet that I shall need Melinda's whopping favorite points for your Dad's faculty. Do not forget that the *top-doggie* administrators in the university need a few bonus points, too."

"Now Daddy, you give Dr. Royce a Zany kiss g'bye, too!" Melinda had more than an inkling that she was an uninhibited, precocious child. She stared at us and gave a melodramatic sigh when Fred and I just laughed.

"And, now my angel, you need to fly upstairs and hop in bed. I shall see Dr. R. out to her car, awesome Baby Azul. I shall be back ASAP to tuck you in bed. Pick out a story and your stuffed animal, honey."

We walked in comfortable silence to my car, Baby Azul. I kerplunked down into a soft leather seat and leaned my arm atop the driver's door.

Fred stooped down at eye level. "Say hi and enjoy your stellar family and simpatico friends in California. Hey, use the sun block," he added, with a wink.

I smiled and flicked my left wrist upward with a thumbs-up sign. I put on my golden-aviator shades, leaned back into my cushy seat, and left the driver's window open. I smiled at Fred and rattled the keys in my right hand.

"Thanks for being an innovative and savvy chair, Fred. Kudos for being a fab Dad, too!"

Fred leaned over closer, so that he could put both hands on the top of my door. He tapped my left shoulder gently, as our eyes met.

"Look forward to our fall semester and that *biggie* limelight. Remember, Dr. Royce? A Fred promise is a promise!"

Flowers furl in the eve, unfurl in a sun-kissed morning,

Relationships bud, blossom, or wither, the atonement of yin or yang,

Fred's promise allowed Dr. Royce an option of choice and change...

MAKE IT
SIMPLE BUT
SIGNIFICANT

Gia and Lee awakened with the beginning of a glorious sunrise,

Cuddled with the aftermath of an amazing-grace sunset,

Hope floated in that bounty of sky artistry...

Come Hither...To Bubbling Brook

"Are you ready for our famous pit stop?" Gia inquired, revealing a mischievous look and her captivating eyes.

"Forever!" Lee responded, intertwining a muscular arm around Gia's slim waist.

They strolled along a familiar footpath bordering the bubbling brook. Both of them treasured these morning walkabouts. Lee's seven-year remission with prostate cancer sustained the welcome bursts of hope and their noticeable moxie.

Lee and Gia would stop for a late breakfast on most weekends. Little did they foresee that today's entertainment was going to be something else.

After years of pit stops at Bubbling Brook Diner, Lee and Gia became convinced. There seemed to be an inner gong. Everyone rushed to the cozy diner, mostly at the same time for the daily yummies.

Perhaps, it was the morning special or a medley of breakfast goodies with a cup of their acclaimed house brew. Seating was the side-by-side chairs or cafe tables, cozy-close to witness the mighty breakfast eaters along with the weekly shenanigans.

There were a few "musts" while waiting, barely hanging on with the delightful aromas and one's hunger pangs. One must eyeball everything that was happening. One must wave wildly for a top off of Bubbling Brook's bold-roast brew. One must insure a sizable dent in his or her empty and wanton tummy with the MAX order of the tempting goodies.

That was about the point where today's intrigue began.

Stuart, nicknamed Cook Supremo by Lee and Gia, was in fifth gear. Good thing, because Teddy was not. Teddy's routine of sorts?

Appear and reappear from the back room with a super-swinging door. Actually, that mastery was a feat, given Teddy's zombie-like stare and a pace to match.

Zippo. Nada. So much for Stuart's daydream for a happy camper or a stellar helper at his grill.

There were several waitresses. Ah, but they did not exactly move in the fast lane either.

"Check out the drama with the waitress scenes, Lee!"

"Not missing a thang, my sweet!"

"Judy might be related to Teddy, ya know!" Gia commented, as she watched the animated entertainment.

"Definite possibility!"

Judy liked to leave via the super-swinging back door as well. She returned whenever. Just one glass of water. She was into "the ones." It was always one pick-up for Judy. Done deal!

After a spellbinding wait, Lee and Gia were seated at an intimate cafe table in the corner. They clinched an incredible view of the lively commotion and the chit-chatting. Entre' another waitress named Mattie.

"Lee, we are the chosen ones. Mattie refilled her ice tea glass from a pitcher near our cushy table, used our sugar with a smile and a wink. Then swished her glass 'round and 'round, adding another heaping mound of sugar. Of course, her distinctive winks at us before dashing away!" Gia exclaimed. "What a *vamoose* exit!"

"Sugar high, eh?" Lee offered, taking hold of Gia's petite hands.

"Hmm, adrenalin rush?" Gia mused, squeezing his hands in that moment. Lee flashed a grin, revealing his adorable dimples. Then they exchanged a notorious look.

"So much for our hunger pangs being appeased sometime today!" Gia stated, unable to stifle a giggle and the teary eyes.

"Hang tough, my love!" Lee jested.

Both of them gave the prominent look again, clasping their hands. Their next winks and closer cuddles were interrupted.

Connie appeared. She was the last of the three dynamos.

"Well, we got to order, ya think," Gia commented, flashing an exotic Cheshire cat grin at Lee.

"Just might be our lucky morning, sweetheart!"

While drinking water and waiting for their yummies, Lee and Gia went back to eyeballing Judy. She was putting on ruby red lipstick, without any mirror. Her contorted faces were amazing, until Mattie demanded their utmost attention. Mattie was performing rather unique aerobics alongside a counter on her way to the other customers.

"Not to worry, Stuart is gaining fame for his feats as well. Lee, I expect to read about *all of them* in the next Guinness Book!" Gia proclaimed. Their ruckus laughs made Gia hang onto her mommy-to-be belly.

"Absolutely! Let's see what is cookin' Hey, no pun…" Lee started to reply, as his voice trailed off when he saw Stuart whizzing in their direction.

With a distinctive flair, Stuart had cooked Lee and Gia's breakfast plus six other piping hot breakfasts with an ASAP personal delivery. Somehow, Stuart had managed to whip up another batch of bold-roast brew for the incoming crowd.

"Hmm, Connie disappeared. Behind the swinging back door? Guess Mattie and Teddy were lonely in that mystical room, Lee."

"They are dreaming up magical recipes for our new specials, sweetheart!"

Later, as Lee and Gia were polishing off their goodies, they witnessed the comical, sink-scrubbing routine. Too much!

"Let's watch this action!" added Gia, as she head-nodded to the nearby sinks. Lee cranked his neck, like an ostrich, to check out the airborne bubbles headed into the cafe.

Judy was quick to pass off the soap-sudsy cleaner to Mattie who protested.

"Oh, please!" Too bad, Judy had already sauntered away, with a rowdy chuckle and those humorous faces.

Oh well, just a few tidbits left to accomplish. Who would help?

"Look! Yep, it is Stuart. This time, he is semi-rescued by guess who? Indeed, it is semi-comatose, Teddy!" touted Gia.

"Yep, Stuart to the rescue...again!" Lee managed to say, between his peals of laughter. Gia and Lee kept laughing hysterically. The noisy crowd with the next arrivals and departures kept them in the safe zone. Yay, not noticed!

Certain customers who happened to be sitting near them got an authentic taste of Teddy's expertise—burnt cinnamon toast and the semi-cooked bacon and eggs. Gia and Lee's bionic eyes were still working. With puckered lips and pinched noses, they remained smitten with today's entertainment.

Both of them continued to stare, but their hysteria was aroused again. This time Gia and Lee hugged longer to muffle the sound effects. Just huggin' lovers at that cafe table.

Gia was reflecting, as Lee and she departed.

We sorta manage to stifle our laughs, given our hug-and-hide cuddles. Too funny! I am going to steal one last glance. But, Lee is giving me that sideway glance and grin, revealing his lovely dimples. I wonder if our baby is going to have the adorable dimples? Our precious moments are not to be taken for granted.

"Nope, thangs have not changed much. Thumbs up and a standing ovation for Stuart, the Cook Supremo!" Gia declared, whenever they finally made their way to the brookside path.

Lee kept grinning and intertwined their arms, as he spoke in a soothing voice. He gestured to an array of flowers along the path leading away from Bubbling Brook Diner.

"Witness nature's gifts, my love. Plus, a rare fortune, our forthcoming gift of a long-awaited baby!" Lee murmured, glancing at Gia's blossoming tummy.

"I am grateful, Lee. All of our *loving* gifts..." Gia's voice trailed off, as she spotted and pointed out a wild, forget-me-not flower.

Lee halted on purpose. "In this moment, I do know TWO...*forget-me-not* earthlings who deserve the applause and a standing ovation!"

Gia paused, nodded thoughtfully, as Lee placed his hand on her mommy-to-be belly. Lee gazed longer into Gia's contented eyes, as the bubbling brook listened to the romantic whispers.

Endless laughter and comedic entertainment at Bubbling Brook Diner,

Welcome changes from an earlier, unsettled world of Lee's remission,

Come hither, experience the life-giving moments of Gia and Lee's steadfast togetherness...

Metaphysical Resonance

No mystery or the bewilderment means a surrender. It was a familiar expression that Seth contemplated at this stage of life. His phrase reinforced a strong belief and a fuller acceptance of the unknown or the unexpected experiences in his life wayfaring.

Seth recalled that his life coincidences happened at the right time and the right place. They were often unexpected. In awe, Seth reaffirmed this possible co-existence. Little did he suspect that today would reinforce that vibrant reality.

Seth had been putting in his contact lenses, when he heard a familiar tune in the background. He dared to scurry towards a music channel on the television. He kept a cupped hand over his right eye, the one without a much-needed contact.

Then Seth heard—in the nick of time—a native American tune. At least he could see well with his left eye. There was beautiful photography along with an inspirational caption. Seth listened to the familiar lyrics, enfolding his mindful heart in that phenomenal moment.

About fifteen years ago, Seth had attended ~~a~~ drumming circle at a non-denominational Unity church. A Native American flutist and singer was offering a Saturday evening for his sacred drumming circle.

Seth respected that sacred drumming circle, just like it happened yesterday. Today, he murmured aloud, as that past scenario returned quickly.

"Only seven of us attended. For whatever reasons, most people chose to attend the Sunday service where Gary was going to sing only two songs during a regular service." Seth paused to refresh today's consciousness.

"I remember that only seven of us attended that evening. The sacred drumming circle resonated powerfully and unexpectedly. I honored and loved my heightened metaphysical awareness, a genuine endowment," Seth added, somehow compelled to keep talking aloud.

"I bought Gary's CD that Sunday, but had not listened to the entirety for a few years. Now, his Native American music was playing on my music channel."

On different occasions, Seth would take a break to appreciate the Native American artists. He rarely heard this genre of music on this channel. Today, the tune triggered a memory of the sacred drumming circle with Gary and the seven kindred beings.

"Any day or time can trigger the powerful memories!" Seth remarked. "Imagine, fifteen years ago and still resonant."

He valued the recollections of his dear friends and a close-knit family who spoke about similar experiences. Seth danced back to his bathroom to put in his much-needed right contact. He had barely finished when another rare tune came forth.

This time Seth was able to scurry quickly to the beckoning tune. Today, another song and a different genre were permitting an unprecedented memory to reappear.

"Wow, that experience was about forty years ago. Phenomenal! And, of course, today's memory lane." Seth did not care that he was still talking aloud. He felt compelled *and* stirred in the same moment.

Yesterday's resonant songs, playing one right after the other, released today's heartfelt feelings. His free spirit was uplifted immediately. Seth returned to dance around his spacious living room.

Suddenly, Seth stopped in amazement. "Just like seven of us danced during and after Gary's sacred drumming circle!" In a few minutes, Seth's stillness and his inner reflections came forth.

None of us predicts the exact timing. Present in a certain moment casts a spellbinding essence. As a floating dance spirit, my earthly time clock is illusive. Yet, I sense in these special moments, that there is an enlightenment.

I scurry to witness, pause, and partake of these two spellbinding songs. Both of them are unexpected flashbacks to other meaningful images of times gone by, yet not. These songs open another door to a vibrant, important renewal—my resounding gratitude and a joyous feeling state to boost today's and tomorrow's creative endeavors.

Inspire a new truth, Seth. That is exactly what I intend to do. Right now…

"A friend, a significant other, a partner, a sibling, or a stranger shares openly. We listen and a valued truth rebounds on a certain day, a regeneration for our soul," Seth recounted, in a warm, vibrant intonation. Then Seth reiterated his spoken conviction, a gratitude for this special day.

"There is nothing as precious in my life journey as these unexpected and resonant memories. Om Shanti."

Always a resonance of a memory lane and taking the risks,

Life was a celebration, no matter what stage of his wayfaring,

Today's acceptance and Seth's inspiration for a new truth was released...

Pink heart chakra underlies an emerald green hue and the feminine of Archangel Raphael,

Witness and foresee a rose quartz healing for Angel Gardenia,

An earth messenger affirms that hope and optimism can co-exist...

Earth Messenger

My self-talk is rarely off base, opening the door to a unique experience. Today's mission, which I choose to accept wholeheartedly, is to buy the just-right cards for my significant others. Their new beginnings are deserving of the acknowledgment and my encouragement.

I find their cards. Or the just-right cards find me expeditiously.

There was only one clerk at a register. Standing there, my eyes connected with a hematite-cross necklace and her name tag.

Our greetings came first, followed by my curiosity. "Wow! Is Angel your real name?" I asked.

Angel laughed heartily. "Oh, indeed! You would not believe the teasing I got growing up, when my full name, Angel Gardenia, was known."

"I can just imagine!"

Our genuine moments enticed an unexpected visiting time. Pretty easy as well, since no customers had shown up.

"I like your name, Angel. It is a perfect combo with Angel Gardenia."

"I agree, especially at this stage of my life. As a child? An adolescent? No way!"

Both of us chuckled knowingly. Still no customers waiting for any check-out line. Angel seemed eager for a longer visit, as she began to share a daily affirmation and her personal leaps of faith.

"I have a spiritual name. My husband does. We decided right away. Name our daughter Serenity. Four times, we have tried to have a child. Three miscarriages and a still-born at eight months. This will be our fifth hope for a blessing."

In that precise moment, our eyes met. The silence and a trance-like stare were not uncomfortable, just natural.

I spoke confidently. "The fifth time. My heart affirms that Serenity needs to come forth. Why? She will be a pure joy to our world as well."

Angel responded rapidly. "Hope so. I figure all of us will have the best-ever names and our family love." Angel's hopes and candor touched a chord within my soul.

"Intentional hopes. Trust and conviction. Acceptance and manifestation, Angel." I found myself underscoring a resilience, much like her voice and the matters of their familial hearts.

She stared at me again. "I shall! I shall choose to believe."

Both of us wished each other a continuous day of splendor. That is exactly what happened for myself. Lustrous minutes arrived the rest of that magical and mystical day. My inner muse was intruding now, in the best of ways.

Hmm, my self-talk returns. I believe that it is destiny, fate, or even no coincidence that Angel Gardenia and my path intersect today. The quiet store is a gift.

As I depart from her store, I feel an immediate flashback. It is a phrase in a spiritual poem that I write and repeat in my daily pathfinding and personal renewals.

"Let my spirit soar." I love when this serendipity touches another individual's lifetime.

Today, I decide to linger with Angel Gardenia. Shared merriment and a genuineness between strangers sets a transcendent tone for my kinder, gentler day.

Later in my travels, I decided to venture into another eclectic store. I read an intriguing feature article. The gargantuan dogs were the first to greet customers. No problem!

I was smitten by dogs, horses, cats and kittens, and truthfully, any sundry critter. No shocker, as I adopted his black Labs in a heartbeat.

"Hiya, big guys. Looking for a playmate?" I asked merrily, as they dropped two balls at my feet.

"You do not have to play, but they would adore even a nudge of their balls with your cool-lookin' boots," the owner countered, with a unique half-grin.

"Sure! Ready, you guys? Go for it!" I spouted in a louder tone, as I nicked each ball with my funky boot tips.

I did roam around his store, in spite of my enchantment and a playtime with his dogs. Several customers had left his store to walk the main street that housed the appealing boutiques.

Meanwhile, the two dogs were content with a grandiose fix of attention from myself. Later, they resorted to being lounge lizards on their mammoth doggie pillows.

The owner and I exchanged dog stories, as I joked about their siesta time. It was obvious that I was enjoying his dogs, but had no purchase in mind. Well, that is what I was thinking in the moment.

I contemplate to myself. No worries. This owner knows the shoppers from the lookers (me, of course!). It is not long before the owner shares his shop talk about the daily visitors.

"You can tell when people come into my store, especially if they are overspending or maxed out on the credit cards. They have fewer smiles. Uptight parents and even their kiddos. They are buying things that they do not need. Hey, they are supposedly on a glorious vacation or a weekend break," he exclaimed, shaking his head in disbelief.

"Uptight and not having fun, eh?" I offered. "Not exactly experiencing the happy-camper minutes, even in this intriguing shop."

"You bet! You are a perceptive human. You nailed it!"

During our conversation, it was his genuineness that made me pay closer attention.

"I think everyone can listen or learn to attend to that voice within or whatever is your belief. Personally, I believe there is a common thread that all religions share. That is where we know what feels right, kind, or what we can try to give back on a given day or a particular week."

"Certain moments affirm what to do or just become the expression of the heartfelt feelings. For me, they just arrive," I added, as both of us paused purposefully.

We had engaging dialogues about our human imperfections and trying to discover life's spiritual paths. Nowadays, it seemed like individuals were desiring a medley of those conscious explorations.

So much for the societal forewarnings: do not engage in any political or religious conversations. Well, no taboos for either of us. When I departed, the two doggies were snoozing in La La Land and the afternoon was disappearing.

Late afternoon, as the sun was setting, I was encircled in a skyline of magnificent hues. Next came a distinct memory of the anecdotes from a movie. I did not know when and where. However, my authentic expression of hopeful thoughts commenced.

Today's shared moments are unpredictable. Yet, it is inspirational to meet a kindred individual who believes in listening to our voice within, no matter what religious denomination or our ancestral, influential beliefs.

Reading that feature article, the intrigue, and my decision for a pit stop makes a space for today's dialogues. None of us predicts how, where, or when a meaningful connection happens.

Later this afternoon, my heart feels the warmth of another positive vibration, as though the experience is right now. Memorex! I believe that it is an exquisite beauty of the afternoon skyline and my nature strolls that bring forth these prized reminisces and my positive feelings.

My thoughts are still roaming, transforming to another special time and place. I am feeling the warmth in my heart.

It was a sister-friend who reminded me of a spirituality on our phone dialogues. I was thanking her for our genuine friendship and the nudges. Olivia was earnest and humble.

Olivia spoke confidently. "I am just a messenger for God. We are all on the same page of the play book."

I was hesitant, thinking that my tough times would result in eviction, even with our kinship of decades. "Have you talked with anyone?" I asked warily.

Olivia laughed in her unmistakable way, then spoke candidly. "No, I have not talked with your sister, parents, or Shawn." By now, she knew that I was crying.

"What makes you think that I would *judge* you?" Olivia asked, with obvious and tender amusement. "Why, if I was there, I would slap your hand with a wet noodle, my endearing friend."

Next? Our glorious hilarity that insured that our tummies would hurt so good.

I recall talking about my pain and the mistakes. And, of course, the perceived judgments to be pronounced—due to my lack or my limitations.

My dear friend knew exactly when and how to respond. "All of us are heavenly children. God is trying to get our attention. Hey, little sheep, will you follow me? Psssssst! It is this beautiful road, not that way. Over here!"

Olivia reiterated a few scenarios, when I remained steadfast and there for her. She consoled me with the poignant memories. The proof? My charger had to be attached to my low-battery cell phone. It would have bleeped out before our marathon dialogues were finished.

Whatever your discarded or held-fast faith, there comes an occasion to pause longer. I knew it, then and now.

Our extensive phone dialogues ensued across the years. Olivia made me laugh each time that we conversed—with the clarity, a loving-kindness, and her trademark sense of humor.

My flashback ensured something else. I did a rereading of my resonant affirmations that heralded our moving-forward momentum. The profound books found me, as much as my eyes feasted upon them.

As I reread the humanitarian writings, I found my Renaissance mentors. Was I accepting or dismissing the miracles in my life? Further readings underscored the inherent value of pursuing who we really wanted to be.

There was a choice to remain curious children or not. The mystery and a mystique in my life had opened the unfamiliar or unusual doors, as if there was a timely cue.

I took the baby steps or felt a surge of faith. Each of my inspirational experiences was an upswing, an definite escalation to enjoy. Before falling asleep, a telepathic message reverberated, as I was drifting off into my alpha-wave dreamscapes.

I wrote my journal entry the next morning. "There is a difference. I am growing older, but I feel wiser. I am becoming an old soul."

Olivia offered her sister-friend a spirituality, an unconditional solace,

Surrender to the trials, a mystery, and the mystique of a life force,

Know a difference between growing older or becoming a wiser soul...

Just Be

My cell phone began its jazzy tune.

"Mom, my cell phone is ringing while I am talking to you. It might be Dad. I have not had an opportunity to chat with him this week."

Juggling my home and cell phones, I was a playful sight. First, my funky dance to grab the cell phone. Second, my attempt to keep talking to Mom on the landline, while attempting to jive wildly across the living room of my log cabin.

During my dah-dah moments, it was my astute Mom at ninety-one years young who came to the rescue. "Sweetheart, answer your cell phone and just call back," she offered, in an endearing tone. "Are you dancing around your log cabin again?" she teased.

"Oh, indeed! You know my funky style. I inherited certain parental-jive genes." After a minute or two, I caught her drift.

Earth to Celine. "Thanks, Mom! Love you!"

I peeked while hanging up my landline phone. As I plopped dramatically onto the couch, the name was not Dad. My assistant minister's name—Pascal—was showing up on my cell phone. His unique name enticed a brain wave or two.

It is a call about our final class. My covenant group with the Wednesday eve class had been meeting for two years.

Bleep. Wrong.

Yet, Pascal did impart a foreshadowing regarding our final class. "I shall be making that call soon, once I get back a few emails. I think it will be the first Wednesday evening in June," he offered.

There is something else. I just know it!

"Oh, I was wondering if you wanted to take part in the service on Sunday? I really do not need an immediate answer." I tuned into Pascal's serene persuasion about the service and its relevance with our class.

I began to half-smile, much like a funny caricature. I adored our covenant group and the spiritual practices that heightened my affinity and stirred the repetitions across the months. There was a phrase that resonated across the entire two years.

Of course, my phrase was a simpatico fit with his last Sunday sermon for the congregation. Pascal and his wife were venturing to Europe to explore their next experiences on the horizon.

I know that Pascal's pause is coming. And, of course, I am going to confide.

"I had a gut feeling that a phone call was forthcoming after our class and your group invitation," I confirmed, letting go with my soft chuckles.

He laughed as well, undoubtedly remembering, as I did. No one in our covenant group had sprung forth with a resounding "Yes!" that evening.

Again, I muse momentarily. Heavens, it is not that any class member is shy or intimidates easily with the idea of participating in his last Sunday sermon. It is a tribute and an honor.

I believe that each of us focuses on the finality of his departure, even though he reassures us that they are returning whenever they are in the area. I recall his exact words.

"Why, I grew up in this church. My family is still here."

"Yes, but..." The group comments followed instantly.

With today's call, I reflected only for a split second. "I shall give you a call later," I responded, not wanting to make my choice with this phone call.

"Sure, Celine! A couple of weeks is fine," Pascal added quickly. We talked a bit longer, ending with our friendly goodbyes. After a few days, I took the liberty and my quality time to muse again.

The nudges for me? Pascal, our assistant minister, owns a superb memory for the spiritual practices that are a keepsake for our covenant group.

Yes, my phrase touches a chord. Hmm, my Celine phrase just happens to fit "simpatico" with his theme for the last sermon. Synchronistic moments? Although a few days pass since Pascal's phone call, my next signs arrive on the scene.

I awakened from a sound sleep. I began to imagine or daydream in my early morning stupor of the possibilities and sharing with our congregation. I would write a Celine story using a creative flair.

I would wing it—standing at the front of our congregation and sharing in the moment. Now, that last image awakened me, eyes wide open.

I was ready with my resounding "Yes!" when the invitation came with Pascal's next phone call. I remembered his kind manner.

"Celine, thank you so much! Take a few minutes. Just share," he offered, as though I had participated regularly in front of our congregation.

It did not matter. Pascal had a way of engaging with people of all ages and backgrounds, putting them at ease, and letting a comfort settle into their interactions.

"Well, I confess. My focus did a u-turn since our last call."

"Fabulous! Am I going to be surprised?" Pascal teased.

"Ah, maybe? My mission, which I choose to accept (sic), is to share my personal experience and my special phrase."

"That would be perfect!" Pascal exclaimed, without saying that he already knew.

"My Celine plunge came to the forefront. Not a *first* in my life time journey. With your phone call, I have another tidbit to relinquish." I paused purposefully.

"I decided to write and read so that you would not be saying, 'cut, cut, and cut' as I headed past a few minutes!" I gave a hearty cackle.

"That tidbit is funny. And, so are you!" Pascal replied, showing his continued appreciation of my candor and a tidbit of Celine's whimsy.

Little did Pascal suspect that I had not only written but also timed my Sunday reading—well, more or less. Then I printed and put away my treasure until that Sunday or so I planned.

Another confession? I reread my script out loud, with no worries on the time factor, smirked, and stashed it in a special drawer. I felt no urgency to rewrite, but I completed my master planning.

I truly believed that God smiled when we humans made our plans, especially a master plan. Well, another inspirational flash hit me.

Sunday is going to arrive. Famous last words. Just remain flexible or whatever when the moments in front of the congregation really arrive. In the interim, my heart feels a pure desire. Turn my minutes into an inspirational short story.

Things change naturally. It is tomorrow. And, it was about doing and being that come readily to my heart. My composition is five or seven minutes. However, I know that my writing continues after this service. I am taking another Celine plunge to write about matters of a pure heart.

Several engaging, nourishing spiritual practices in our covenant group still resonate. In the next year or so, my undivided attention is on my personal reminisces and an evolution of my writings. For now, my thoughts return to our covenant group.

Our nourishing practices came from highly respected books. Pascal would read passages from the different metaphysical sources. Companion and heartfelt videos left the astounding imprints.

My Celine practice permitted a slow-down-and-absorb pace, something akin to a giant sponge. Soak up a word, the phrase, or a quintessential sentence. Let this practice nourish my being. Immerse and digest slowly.

No problem! Hey, I was a very slow eater, as my family and friends would attest, without further ado. Almost literally, I would chew slowly, letting a phrase nourish my being. Today, I need to recall these gifted years in our covenant group.

What words, resounding phrases, or special sentences gain my attention effortlessly and go straight to my heart? Given our time and open space, the classes fill my cup with the spiritual phrases for an entire lifetime.

Resonant phrases become the diverse mantras with my meditative practices. I meditate daily, intertwining a gifted phrase with my ancient healing practices. I want to keep reflecting about these earlier spiritual journeys.

Spiritual pauses, my reprieves, and an ultimate renewal. My whole being remains delighted. I am paying closer attention.

It came as no shocker as to why I elected to join our covenant group with the spiritual practices. These years became my personal reprieve, a special moment on Wednesday evenings. Our covenant group happened throughout our longer fall foliage, numerous wintry Nor'easters, and two of the earliest, welcoming springs.

Our group was experiencing the metaphysical writings and the re-awakenings in these covenant gatherings. We spoke candidly, respecting only the covenant group for the precious stories.

Our generic one-liners were fine to pay forward. I reread my notes and spoke aloud to recapture the striking individuality and wealth in our group.

"In a whirling dervish world, oodles of personal memories are *not* seeking eviction."

"Glimpses of our past or the future are not suspect."

"Any of us depletes the quality time and at least a tank of energy when we hang tight to our intrusive or even obsessive ego. Be gone!"

"Hey, that racing-thoughts syndrome that is fine with our intrusive egos? Mind chattering and cluttering? All of us here can and do strive to declutter. Our ego truly needs to take a break!"

The group responded with their appreciative laughter, immediate head nods, and vibrant hand claps with our commentaries and the insights.

Flash. Another news bulletin arrived. I discovered myself writing differently. Now, I was tweaking my Celine ideas for the service. I also stretched to tweak and reread aloud— my inspirational quests from my published book.

"Tune in. Change the channels, if need be."

"Release often."

"Stop. Take three longer breaths. Adios to the shallow breaths."

"Practice the self-love. Unconditional love will blossom."

"Stop chasing life. Inner peace will visit each of us."

My ideas were coming full circle. This weekly tweaking of diverse ideas and the musings prompted something else.

I was already anticipating and savoring our upcoming Sunday service. I knew when I wrote my phrase. "My soul is open to being and becoming."

I found myself repeating my Celine gift—slowly. I read my written phrase—slowly. When I walked or paused in a moment, my written phrase came back—slowly. When meditating, my written phrase came full circle—slowly.

It was not long. I became mindful of my written phrase. It brought forth an evolving sacred place and an inner peace.

My choice was to explore that sacred place, even if it was only seconds or a few minutes. "Just be," I would declare aloud.

That Sunday service did arrive. The assistant minister, our congregation, and I attended *and* listened—Celine's moment of moments.

I took my seven minutes and Celine's compelling stories of moving forward—not backward. There was a quality of time for unveiling my truths.

Before ending, I paused to look around at our congregation. Turning slowly towards Pascal, I spoke confidently.

"My soul is open to being and becoming."

HELLO
PEOPLE NICE
TO MEET YOU!

Pascal offered an awareness of the spiritual realms and the environmental stepping stones in a life journey,

Celine and the covenant group pledged to fine-tune their affirmations for a worldly harmony,

Synchronicity and rejuvenations became a welcome greeting at these covenant doors of understanding...

Transformations

Amber Seaberg-Santillo had been attending an online healing summit this past week featuring a medley of renowned leaders. The contemporary findings in epigenetic studies, neuroscience, and the metaphysical realms were fascinating. It was a glorious week of opening and expanding one's mind, body, and spirit.

The last month, Amber was engaged in writing a beloved memoir about her partner. This evening, she took a longer respite to cook a splendid dinner. She poured a glass of wine and lounged on her couch. The sudden resurgence of a transformative energy from her memoir writings, the profound summit, and the liberating voices of the professionals happened in a nanosecond.

One inspirational session was entitled, "Our place of breathing called euphoric Hope Village." The presenter emphasized the intrinsic worth of a simplistic phrase or a mantra in concert with one's soulful meditations. This session paralleled Amber's training, current clients, and her ongoing practices in the ancient healing realms and the eclectic meditations.

Tonight, Amber chose to write spontaneously in a brand-new journal. She coveted a strong belief in the new beginnings.

Brand-new endings could also emerge for her partner who was on the same wave length. Positive intentions for their transformations were composed.

Amber's pen moved effortlessly across the first page. Free-flowing writing was her style. Tonight revealed a nostalgic and hopeful phrase—just ask—one that resounded across the decades.

Just ask…
Archangel Gabriel heralds our highest good and a life force,
Copper trumpet raised to the ethereal realms,
Archangels Raphael and Michael meld an emerald-hue healing with a purple and the royal blue protections,
Archangel Jophiel bequeaths a golden aura and a coaxing of the feminine energies,
All guardian and archangels usher in the strong vibrations for our spiritual connection.

Just ask…
All witnesses to my transformation and an evolution of spirit,
Awakening my human being in the moments of now,
Gifting my human being with the cloud personifications, the sky art, and my rainbow-bridge messages,
Filling my human being with a soulful abundance from a timely summit,
Composting with a memoir of giving and receiving—to my simpatico, gifted partner and to our new, escalating world called Hope Village.

Mirror images cleansed a window to Amber's soul, opening her to this summit of metaphysical, neuroscience, and epigenetic realms,

Learning to give and receive not only for her simpatico, valued partner but also for our new world,

This transformative energy prevailed for Amber Seaberg-Santillo...

Four...Not Three

She let the phone ring, knowing that he was slow to stand up and walk, using his mahogany, handcrafted cane. There were never any complaints, a rehashing of the past burdens.

Katrina was five when his two ruptured discs, serious surgeries, and bedridden became his world. A fierce willpower and steadfast healing were his paths, unexplainable and respected with his humbled doctors and the caregivers.

"Happy Birthday, *Daddy!"* Katrina sang out with a quirky, musical rendition. I treasure that you are seventy-seven. Seven is my favorite number, so my prediction?" Katrina paused, only for a few seconds.

"Daddy, your double sevens are a jackpot. A golden abundance, right? Best of the BEST, my love, and enormous hugs are coming to YOU, dear Daddy—zooming across the 2,000 miles!"

"Thanks, honey!" he expressed. "Love you, Katrina. Can't wait to see you at Thanksgiving!" continued Dad, in his jovial voice.

"Me, too! Start the countdown, Daddy!" Katrina expressed with excitement. "Now, listen carefully. Sometime, during this special day, you will feel my presence."

"Katrina, I shall feel your *fabulous* presence all day!"

"Lots of love, Daddy! Call ya in a few days."

"Bye. I know you are off to school soon. Lots of love to you *and* those kiddos!"

"Thanks! Hugs galore and my generous, affectionate vibes. Bye, Daddy!"

Katrina zoomed down her stairs, heading off to school with plenty of energy. She was darn ready for story time and her exceptional kiddos.

"Are all of you *excited* to hear the title of today's story?" Katrina asked, using her melodramatic flair.

"Yes, Ms. Katrina! Oh, yes!"

"Right now, please! Oh, pretty please, Ms. Katrina."

"We know it is going to be the BEST story!" Seven of Katrina's kiddos even had their hand claps and head nods in sync.

"Ready? Are you sure? Here comes the title. Four...Not Three!" Ms. Katrina declared, in a bold and enticing voice. Ms. Katrina used her long, slender fingers when she stated those numbers and began the story.

There were a loving mother and father who had three VERY CURIOUS children. You bet! They knew that they were loved.

BUT...their mother kept wanting one more child. Well, this worried the father. The mother had health problems, so a fourth child? Oh my, the worries kept creeping into this Dad's loving heart.

That summer, the loving mother and father decided. Joseph joined his forever-friends, the three sisters who adored his cooing, bubble-smiles, and big-time burps.

Whoosh! Time flew....

The end of the lumber yard became a favorite playground, much to their parents' dismay. For each of them, the JUNKY wood piles in the lumber yard held outstanding treasures!

Grammy and Gramps visited with treats, homemade breads with real butter, and tons of hugs. They even chased off their playmates, Howie and Kris, whenever they messed up the flower beds and herbs, right near the front porch.

Sabrina took special delight running next door and shouting, "Grammy and Gramps, they jumped around all of our flowers and herbs again!" Sabrina loved to watch and tummy-giggle, especially whenever Grammy and Gramps chased off the boys.

Now, these four children adored their Dad and Mom. Yes, they were there—for the neighborhood bird funerals, fixing colorful scooters and bikes, the family picnics, and getting lost on all the country drives and adventures.

Can you believe that Joseph got a nickel when he got his finger smooshed in the car door on one adventuresome trip? He did!

Wow, big changes were happening. They were moving and beginning a new adventure. They got a dog, a kind and slobbering Great Dane named Voodoo. Each kid fell into the packing boxes of the movers, almost getting hauled away.

There were lots of playmates at the new home. Golden Thunderbolt, a lively stallion, lived next door.

"I want to ride that wild horse," bellowed Joseph. "I shall for sure!" he declared at the dinner table. All of his sisters knew that Joseph meant every word. So did his parents.

"Now, Joseph..." Mom and Dad replied, always in the same breath.

Oh, how Sabrina and Joseph loved sneaking into that forbidden pasture. Golden Thunderbolt was wild, rearing up and pawing the air with his hoofs. Then he would race after them. Each time they made it under the fence and back into their yard, giggling and trembling.

Mom and Dad made a neat friend next door. He had a classic Thunderbird car with lots of chrome. Bling, Bling!

It was a harder school system for all of them, but they made friends easily. They got smarter in this school as well.

Whoosh, time flew...

Lakeside summers with longer vacations meant handsome beaus for all the girls and a gorgeous girlfriend for Joseph.

"Ugh, quit teasing us, Dad!" Joseph said, trying to stifle his laughs.

"Oh, deep inside, all of us truly love the attention, Dad and Mom!" admitted Sabrina, one evening when they were cooking on the grill.

"Just pulling your legs," Dad would say, especially to Sabrina.

"Oh sure, Dad. That is why my legs are so-o-o long!" Sabrina would retort.

By high school and college, Dad and Mom became their special friends. They were there for ALL of the ups and downs. Always there—for their dreams AND mighty adventures.

Whoosh, time flew…

Three women and a young man were gazing at the family album. Mom and Dad raised some kooky kids. KOOKY GOOD! The funny photos revealed their awesome sibling playtime and love.

Sabrina adored her family. Now, she had to travel from New Mexico, usually on holidays or her vacations. The trips were priceless. Few people owned or took the quality time to create these kind of unexpected, new, and heartfelt memories.

Across the years, there was a conscious choice. Yes, indeed! Sabrina's mad money was spent for these unforgettable trips.

Her family cracked up with the Sabrina's "mad money" lingo. Few regrets. Well, that promise was a long time ago. Sabrina's few regrets were true-blue.

The family anticipated their new joys. They became magical moments and imagery that Sabrina recaptured back in New Mexico. With each visit, a family playfulness, the dialogues, and a genuine caring touched her heart. Sabrina often repeated what her Mom and Dad had decided. Four…Not Three!

"YAY, Four…Not Three!" shouted Ms. Katrina, waving her four fingers wildly.

Ms. Katrina gazed 'round and 'round the cozy circle of her cherished kiddos. Her students were joyous, holding up and waving four fingers, and then clapping loudly.

"Ah, so you *liked* my story, huh?" Ms. Katrina said confidently, as she jumped up and did a hilarious dance. Putting her hands on her slender hips, Ms. Katrina stopped suddenly. Ms. Katrina stared at each of them with a huge grin and a few laugh snorts.

They laughed hysterically and kept clapping. Several kiddos were starting to practice Ms. Katrina's laugh snorts. They were ready for everything now.

"C'mon, everyone. Rise up! Release your very special ENERGY. Let's *dance*!" Ms. Katrina announced, showing off her rhythm, flailing long arms and legs, and her contagious excitement. "Let's do a boogie-woogie dance!"

A young kiddo, born into a family of four with the quintessential moments, worth far more than any Princess or Prince's gold,

Like the free-spirit buffalo families, Katrina's growing years were influenced by her nurturing parents and colorful teachers,

Katrina paid forward this energy, an impassioned storytelling, and a contagious dance-vibe with her admiring students...

Secret Muses

Morning reflections and random thoughts in a trance-like space was a daily practice. Natasha began the affirmations and thoughts that she had penned.

I believe... People with an optimistic attitude live longer than those who focus on the pessimistic outlooks. Fewer worries or less judgements. I create a wake-up call for each day and a reflective practice.

Hmm, today's affirmation? I know for sure. I affirm to keep my head out of the sand!

Actually, I enjoy each day and this ownership of my positive attitude and a befitting affirmation. I accept and entrust the highly recommended and daily doses of intentional optimism.

In the last decade, Natasha was more conscious of the science and art of becoming more mindful. She witnessed several fun-loving and caring individuals having a splendid time. Natasha's learning curves and attitude soared with these upbeat scenarios. She became quite attentive and reread the news flashes.

It was in our favor health-wise to be resourceful, searching, seeking, and sustaining a jovial quality of life. A sense of humor and laughter lowered our blood pressure. Actually, they were a generous massage to our vital organs.

There were obvious reasons to be courageous and say a forceful "no" to a daily overabundance of certain expressions. I should, I ought, or I must do. The latest fanfare regarding owning a sense of humor, the outlooks linked to optimism, and an essence of well-being was indeed a far better and healthier reality.

Natasha picked up her cell phone. She decided to call her dearest friend, Darlene. She would be at home this weekend.

"Hey, woman, so fabulous to hear from you!" Darlene shouted over the music. "Yep, I cranked up the music and was dancing while putting away a ton of laundry. Let me crash on the couch and turn down the volume. So, what's up?"

"Just made a perfecto pact with myself. Stay open to wit, charisma, and playful desires within my heart. You know why?" Natasha quizzed, unable to contain a few chuckles.

"Why? I am clueless, Natasha!" Darlene declared, using a raspy voice with her renowned teasing inflections.

"Well, my dearest, my commitment will embellish the untold opportunities for great things! Indeed, like bursts of creative juices, higher peaks and fewer valleys, and get this—a lessening of the bad-to-the-bone distress," claimed Natasha. She only paused a split-second.

"Bad juju, that personal distress! Produces nasty toxins within our mind, body, and soul. How 'bout that, my dearest friend?"

"Vamoose! Whoosh! JuJu begone!" Darlene announced pronto.

Both of them howled, hooted, and giggled—until their tummies hurt real good. They never took for granted that they were the best-ever friends since preschool days.

"Darlene, I was doing a healing summit for a week, picking out the international and national pioneers in the metaphysical and holistic realms. The summit included the neuroscientists, super epigenetic and quantum physics leaders adding the spiritual connections, and other mentors. Many of them affirmed the research that we human beings hang tight and linger with our mediocre or distressful days, weeks, or even months. We pay too much heed to our harried, whirling-dervish world."

"Hey, Natasha. No wonder, no mystery, or dah-dah moments as to why both of us commit to stop each day to find or create our laughs and the joys," Darlene added. "We maintain our sanity in a sometimes insane or bonkers world of angst, the utmost chaos, and the surreal fears."

"Over the decades we have paused together to refresh our self-worth and our unconditional love during the toughest journeys as well," Natasha added quickly. "Not just playtime, but the tough times, Darlene."

Both of them chatted longer and enjoyed the updates. As always, they signed off with love, radiant light, and a promise to talk again.

After Natasha hung up, her younger sister Avanti popped into a consciousness.

Avanti was another significant person and caregiver during Natasha's tougher journeys. Natasha was living in the beautiful hill country of Texas when she was blindsided by health challenges. Natasha began to relive the splendid images of two sisters, much like a technicolor movie that you wanted to watch again and again.

Those unforgettable months of caregiving and the sponge baths that were a surprise or tickled our fancy. I decided ASAP. Ms. Oops became Avanti's nickname.

With or without her bifocals, Avanti tackled the challenge of shaving my wicked long legs. 'Round and 'round my kneecaps, trying not to leave nicks. Shortly thereafter, we decided to name my leftover hairs. These precious images and dialogues returned, just like yesterday. Right now, I can and will recreate those best-ever sister stories!

"Why, it is the grasslands again!" spouted Avanti, pretending to be miffed. "Imagine that sprouting happening? Hmm, I must be Ms. Oops with my bifocals!"

Natasha had smiled, the best she could with the exotic tremors. Later on, she was able to sit in bed for very short intervals and work remotely.

"Hey sis, just call from your bed. Here, gopher-gopher!"

Both of them had giggled, particularly when Avanti (a.k.a. Ms. Oops) would endeavor to mimic a gopher critter. Today's image of Ms. Oops coming into the bedroom with the hilarious antics remained so vivid.

Across the months, their talks were soulful. Mini-strides in Natasha's health translated to the short rides and her gradual walking. Avanti's unconditional love and mother-hen persona co-existed nicely.

"Ok, enough for today, my overkill sister!" Avanti would announce, whenever she decided that enough was enough. "You do *not* know when enough is enough, but I do. C'mon, my tough cookie. Back home, we go!" Avanti would declare with a bigger-than-life embrace.

Natasha would chuckle again. Brief rides and Natasha's gradual walks were off the charts. Any grand jury would concur. Avanti was petite with short legs, trying hard to drive Natasha's stout pick-up.

Stealth Rod, its precious namesake, was bought by the long-legged Natasha. But Avanti? Seat far forward, looking like she was upon Stealth Rod's dashboard when she drove, Avanti was a sight to behold.

"Step on it, Avanti. You gotta merge into our wild traffic!"

"Natasha, I am. I am! My foot is pressed down as far as my petite, short legs can reach. Hang-g-g on, sis!"

It was only later when they laughed about the blaring horns and the BAD looks that they mimicked so well. Other days, Avanti gopher-gopher would drive Stealth Rod to Natasha's workplace. Parking and getting out of the pick up was another melodrama.

"Yikes! I heard screeching, Natasha. I walked up your windy hillside and one of two mockingbirds dive-bombed me. I dropped your tote, picked up the papers galore, ducked another dive-bomber, and made a beeline to the door."

"Ahhh, brave sister. Safe and somewhat sound! A genuine thank YOU!"

Another week was a short ride to visit a western store for Avanti's souvenirs while Natasha rested. Stealth Rod was parked near a storage building, small trees, and a few bushes. While resting, Natasha spotted IT.

"Oh no," Natasha had mumbled. Then she tried to point upward, outside her window. However, Avanti was intent on her keepsakes, waving a handful of bags and smiling proudly.

Meanwhile, Natasha saw IT checking out Avanti's every move. Natasha reached over and started Stealth Rod. Natasha recalled mumbling, "Gotta get outta here!"

Avanti took a longer time opening the door, stopping to show Natasha the souvenirs. Avanti was standing directly in the beeline—the attack zone of you know who.

"Cmon, let's get outta here. You can show me at home," Natasha shouted, as Avanti looked wide-eyed at her. Natasha pointed upward, squinting in the sunlight.

"What? Oh NO, I see. *Another* mockingbird!"

"Man, IT might just decide to dive bomb you!" Natasha declared. Both of them broke into gales of laughter, totally forgetting to look at the souvenir bags from the western store.

"Look at that nest near the shrubs and tree. Right near our parking space and your Stealth Rod. Undoubtedly, we are *prime* targets!" Avanti shrieked, cracking up again.

Once Avanti flew back home, their prime-time calls continued. While Avanti was gone, her hubby had planted a flourishing garden with a scarecrow to boot.

Guess who owned the garden? Natasha believed that Avanti's garden was the crowning sign. A mockingbird arrived on their home turf, just for a nostalgic reminder.

Their next phone call, Natasha blurted out, "Beware, my sister!"

Natasha went back to today's ruminating story and the verbatim recollections. All of us deserved these diversions, sentimental memories, and our enthusiastic renewals. Time-out for claiming former playtimes and the amazing joys became a top priority.

Natasha was grateful for these vibrant memories, as her younger sister died unexpectedly at forty-four. Damn! Breast cancer arrived, dive-bombed into Avanti's life, exactly like those mighty, indomitable mockingbirds.

Natasha's personal bereavement knew no time line. She wrote prose and journaled to keep Avanti's spirit close to her daily life and any daring adventures.

Natasha could not pinpoint the specific day or a month. Finally, she found herself celebrating Avanti's spirit. Natasha felt peace in her heart. Another month, her inner and outer smiles started to reappear.

Layers of solace appeared when Natasha paused to view certain photos or talked about Avanti's caregiving and hilarious times with family, her friends, or even strangers. Somehow, during that toughest-ever time period, there was a rejuvenation of her playful spirit. Natasha felt terrific with today's affinity and the sentimental reflections.

Natasha felt a sudden urge to call a treasured friend in Canada. Nikki was full of spunk and a contagious spirit like Avanti. They met on a cruise for singles about five years ago.

"Nikki, I have been meaning to call ya. Wassup, my soul-sister?" Natasha quizzed, letting a softer, teasing tone slip out.

"Well, hello my daring diva! I am going to have a few weeks off. Thought I might go on a cruise, but I need a roommate? Do ya know who would be wacky and daring enough to room with me?" Nikki quizzed, letting a teasing tone slide right back.

"Me!"

"You are *serious*, Natasha?"

"Yep!"

"Well, you just made my day! Timing is EVERYTHING!"

"Let's do it. Life is too short. Let us live our next defining and outlandish, crazy ventures together!"

"I shall email you with an attachment. Of course, you will need to book a flight to Canada. The rest is my treat!" Nikki declared, dismissing Natasha's protests.

"Now, get online and soar here in the next week. You can begin by hanging up. Text me soon, my soul-sister!"

"Will do. I am psyched! G'bye for now..." Natasha added, as she heard Nikki's last hurrahs and the snapping fingers. She envisioned Nikki dancin' and zigzaggin' around her quaint bungalow.

Natasha pranced and danced like a crazed diva over to her computer. Immediately, she knew. Someone else was adoring this upcoming adventure. Before Natasha went online, she paused to envision and muse—about the *three* divas.

No worries! Avanti, my soulful spirit, you are coming along for this special cruise. I am celebrating you throughout Nikki's and my golden journey on this cruise. So glad to sense your presence, see the vibrant images of our yesterdays, and treasure our jovial tears.

Today, I still envision our twinkling eyes. Avanti, you are holding your tummy from our antics and hysteria. Feeling so fine, so divine. Hey Avanti, I am making another pact with myself.

My daily intention? Never forget our sisterhood legacy. Such abundant laughter, our unconditional love, and the wild-women playtime are my honoring of YOU.

Avanti, my guardian and soaring angel, you are ALWAYS welcome to tag along on ALL of my adventures. Nikki is so on board (sic) for this upcoming cruise and the heavenly adventures. C'mon, Avanti!

AWAY FROM
THE CITY

Reunions, globe-trotting buddies, and a cherished friendship,

Natasha and Nikki planned divine cruises, far away from any city hype or distractions,

Plus their guardian angel Avanti always reigned supreme...

Passion

Phoenix let her passion exude its beacon of light whenever the slivers of darkness appeared or even prevailed during a particular week or an unexpected month. She knew her lineage and valued the symbolism.

"Hmm, I like my name of Greek origin. Better than like. Actually, I love that my namesake symbolizes a rebirth or an immortality," Phoenix told her precious partner.

They cuddled deeper into the soft sheets, making love during a crescent moon—turned uniquely like a beseeching smile—peeking through their window panes. In the wee hours of the morning, Phoenix murmured to her sleeping lover.

"We take deeper breaths to release any of the invasive, recurring thoughts. We follow our breath pattern. Inhale and exhale ever so slowly. Let these breaths flow purposefully to our inner quietude—together."

That morning, there was a sunrise to behold. They witnessed a kaleidoscope of colors followed by the subtle hues. A transformative energy of their partnership arrived quickly.

Effortless love again. Perhaps, a vapor of the divine enfolded them. Before their shower, they cuddled again. In that exact moment, Phoenix felt compelled to whisper their truths.

"We let each moon, a sunrise, or the sunset manifest a pure bliss in our beloved re-awakenings. Together, we release to the next moments and savor our passion."

Phoenix's mirror image of LOVE was always powerful,

Intertwining, these two, translucent-light beings,

The caring whispers and their souls melding together...

Awaken Suspended Memoirs

The oasis of emotions morphed into a mystic calling. These awakenings and a sensation of bliss felt extraordinary. Roth cherished a quality time for the daily meditations and his deliberate, resounding contemplations.

These purposeful interludes were non-negotiable. They permitted an unforeseen door to open completely. The hiatus and a breathing space allowed a different or an untapped reign of Roth's free spirit to be surrendered. The releases were always forceful, dynamic, and persuasive.

An authentic realm of receiving, one that bequeathed his wealth without a price tag, was a serendipitous awakening. The synchronistic wayfaring continued to amaze Roth each day, liberating parts of his suspended memoir.

Shading his hazel eyes, Roth looked upward at today's cotton-candy clouds and a brilliance of sapphire prisms from the sunbeams. He relished this solace, especially since life took its twists and turns—no blindsided him—in a mere two years. Roth recollected that rollercoaster of unforgettable emotions in the company of today's thoughts.

Not sure exactly where and when my cries for an inner peace happened. My cycles of plentiful denials, my festering anger, an illusive bargaining, and my bouts of depression seemed endless.

Finally, my acceptance emerges like the ebb and flow of the bayside tides near my home. I remember feeling less despair and more comfort.

Now, I am able to accept and forgive completely without a depression, without the paralyzing fears, and without the angst of those two-year flashbacks.

Roth's Mom, Dad, and a younger brother were killed instantly by a drunk driver. Every step of the legal pursuits sucked. His partner of fifteen years left him, no longer in love. Roth found his partner's note on a treasured cafe table from their travels to Sorrento and Positano in Italy.

"Any dialogue is null and void. Counseling is *not* an option for us. My heart is empty of our love, only a darkened cavern now."

It was three years later. Roth's continuous meditations on a soft blanket, gazing intermittently at the ocean, and the welcoming imprint of each day caused his distinctive tingles. These new vibrations within Roth's being arrived. No mystery as to why his gratitude became an understatement.

His inner spirit was finally evolving. Roth sensed that a spirit team was in the making, always on his behalf.

Roth knew at this point in his life journey. He would pay forward to the world, unleashing the ripples of hope, the pursuits of forgiveness, and his daily acts of kindness. Roth murmured in that exact moment of his total understanding.

"My slow fuse was lit again during my life journey. How incredible was that offering? Indeed, I shall untie my ribbon for today's gift. I believe and trust this endowment. Each week, I envision the light-filled, gifted moments."

Today, Roth's meditation and his deeper, purposeful breaths had just started. An inner stillness arrived with his continuous "Om" and "Sat Nam" mantras.

Amazing benevolence! A spirit of loving-kindness enfolded Roth's grateful being.

Roth sang a Sanskrit song to celebrate. Here came a splendid re-awakening of the rest of his suspended memoir.

Roth's losses of Mom, Dad, and a younger brother,

Abandonment of a partner, scarring his heart again,

Today, Roth sang a Sanskrit song to heal, to re-awaken, and to create a forgiving, new memoir...

The Sisterhood Radiance

The two sisters, Annalise and Micaela, mirrored an unmistakable radiance. Across the decades, the radiance of their kindred connections was witnessed by significant others and even strangers.

The sisters entrusted an unmistakable super-charge, particularly in the last five years. New-found hills, unmarked or exotic winding trails, and Mother Nature's unforeseen and electrifying vistas on conservation lands were a part of the uplifting gifts.

Their unexpected exchanges with an appreciative stranger, the indulgent dialogues as caring sister-friends, and an exchange of a splendid photo or fun texts happened. Awe and a genuine curiosity emerged on each hiking adventure. They imprinted a particular second, several minutes, or the hours that neither Annalise or Micaela took for granted.

"Wow. The magnificent day and our bequeathed riches. A narrow hiking trail with another paradisio! Fabulous, my enthused and loco sister, Annalise."

"My shining light and love honor today's paradisio! And *funky* you, Micaela. Forever," added Annalise, flashing her pearly white grin.

"Can you believe that hoot owl actually answered our human hoots? Okay, the first hoot. Our other sounds were ignored. That hoot owl flew out of a majestic pine tree for us to witness!" Micaela remarked, giving Annalise an elbow nudge that started the famous laugh-snorts and semi-wheezes of her younger sister.

"Let's come back to this meadow at sunset during the next month. I bet that hoot owl will reappear, just for us!" claimed Micaela. Incredible how those laugh snorts eased Annalise's angst on certain days. Her twin daughters had reached their adulthood, but were not so mature in an array of relationships.

Unmistakable moments like the hoot owl and a discovery of snow-drop flowers during an unexpected snow squall provided another day of a shared splendor. They took ownership of this medley of surprises, the splendor, and their light beams of potential. That elixir of potential and possibility was authentic for these exuberant sister-friends.

One evening, the youngest sister heard a song with relevant lyrics. The time was 11:11 p.m. Micaela knew and texted her endearing sister. "There is a new dimension, our patient waiting on a miracle—for us and our world." She contemplated for a few minutes and continued her text.

"We have tuned into life and living across the decades," Micaela wrote. "Miracles can and do happen—for us and our world." She sent off this text into the cyber world.

Annalise reread Micaela's compelling text. At the bong of midnight, she waited to hear a cyber-touch message zoom back to her sister. With this return text, Annalise let the happy tears stream down her cheeks.

"Just like our golden years as longtime sister-friends. Still alive and kicking with the personal valleys and peaks in life, we are! Our sisterhood radiance reigns supremo. And, of course, the honoring of our potential miracles—for us and our world. Always our legacy of love and a celestial jubilee in tonight's dreams, Micaela."

The sister bonds and travels of Annalise and Micaela tenured an unmistakable radiance,

Humorous adventures, their effortless dialogues, and a bestowal of an expansive love,

Awareness and value of their historic and contemporary sisterhood and a lifetime bond happened for a reason...

Nani

"You gifted me with Aolani, my namesake. What an enticing and alluring name, one that attests to a heavenly cloud in our heritage. My close friends remind me of my unique Hawaiian and inner beauty—Nani!" Those were the expressive and exact words that Aolani conveyed lovingly to her parents last weekend.

"Nani—beauty in our Hawaiian heritage—is authentic," Aolani uttered softly. Then she drifted into a stunning, utopian slumber in her familiar childhood bedroom.

Aolani appreciated that she was born in Hawaii, especially during her Italian and Ireland travels as an avid tour guide. She was passionate about these tours in the late spring, the summer months, and throughout the early fall.

Her professionalism and an affection for touring were obvious. Yet, Aolani's heart always welcomed Hawaii as her home. There was a distinctive serenity about the Hawaiian culture and Aolani's family lineage.

Aolani was a confident woman whose best friends and colleagues declared her to be amicable, very inspirational, and a quirky individual. Her life was sprinkled with the strifes, a share of real crescendos, yet they never robbed Aolani of her inner resilience and a return to a conspicuous self-confidence.

Aolani was at peace when she dialogued with diverse individuals as a fervent tour guide. Whenever she took any reprieves for a joyful and cherished playtime, that inner peace reappeared. Honoring and contemplating out loud was Aolani's weekly ritual for the majority of her life's pathfinding.

"Peace messages enfold our core being, if we choose. Just be tranquil and harmonious. As a child, I commemorate and relive that my parents taught me to pause, remain aware, and summon up a sense of loving peace. They encouraged a natural practice and those tranquil feelings to become an amazing ebb and flow throughout my life span. They shared exquisitely. Those were *generous* lessons for a young girl, a maturing woman, and for my esteemed brothers, Akamu and Koa."

Aolani knew something else. She always gave the reverent bows and the minutes of an inner stillness to the centuries of spirituality. Ancient wisdom was lauded.

Aolani permitted her slower breaths to emerge. These moments heightened a purity of stillness within her mind, body, and spirit. Inner thoughts came forth.

Seek a solitude during a late dusk to the twilight. Scan the majestic skies, yearning to catch a splendor of the moonbeams. The moon's waxing to waning energies bring forth a formidable essence to all of our humanness.

Look up the time and date. Write down my new moon intentions and savor that positivity of going forward. Look up a different time and date. Surrender my Aolani intentions as my positive manifestations during each full moon.

I do not forget the sublime offerings, the online venues, and an insightful or a meaningful workshop. I choose to pause and recapture my quintessential essence and that significance. Then...just be peaceful.

Aolani valued this entirety, a processing and her evolution. She treasured the mellow ebb and flow. She had learned that a legacy evolved, particularly when we humans attended to the moon cycles, given their historic and astrological connections.

The lunar cycles of each moon beckoned our earthly consciousness and a positive mindset. Historic philosophers were reread. The renowned facilitators of the healing summits during a personal or our global crisis affirmed the historic and contemporary inheritance. Aolani valued this vast knowledge and an integration for a progression of her personal legacy.

Aolani reread the persuasive and stirring notes in her daybook. They were a poignant chronicle of the unruffled moments to retrieve the reciprocal learnings.

Today, Aolani nestled into her soft-cushioned chair and its ottoman on a screened porch with the gifted tropical plants. She read the fetching insights in her daybook for her glorious flora, fauna, and her dainty kitten, Eleu.

She read her insights for today's plentitude. And, to enhance the profusion of becoming. Then Aolani grinned at adorable Eleu and continued her inner reflections.

As human beings, it is a solace to pursue our willingness to appreciate this phenomenon of our moon cycles. An inner calm emerges as we humans become discerning and more savvy about the impressive discoveries of these lunar cycles.

An unequivocal abundance and a prosperity arrives with my synchronistic moments. I welcome this personal happiness and my well-being in these mystical moments of co-existence, peace, and harmony.

Aolani honored her Hawaiian heritage. She summoned to mind that inner beauty with one treasured word.

"Nani!" intoned Aolani.

Be strong. Conquer from within. Know thyself,

Aolani was peaceful, appreciating her beautiful heritage.

Nani–came full circle again...

Angelic Whisperers And Messengers

Deta had taken the workshops, trained and mentored in England, and read a multitude of credible books the past decade. There was a readiness and an excitement for the diverse personas that would grace her event during this two-day summit.

"When Angels Show Up in Your Life" was pitched as the hook for today's international summit. She wondered if the diverse participants would be hooked. Whatever peaks and valleys appeared throughout this day, Deta felt a surge of willingness and an inspiration run the gamut with her Aussie verve.

"Deta, take a quick peek through this side of the stage curtain. A fabulous crowd is showing up for your angel event," Roland exclaimed, giving an affirming pat on her shoulders. Even as Deta's new agent, he was not surprised.

"Hey, no worries or nervousness? That is a full auditorium and almost an hour earlier than my scheduled event, Roland. Not getting too cocky until—the majority of them *really* engage."

The opening moments and an anticipation created the inner butterflies. Deta knew immediately.

Deta walked gracefully, her long-legged and trim body in a beguiling outfit. The outfit matched her presence and a vibrant persona. Soon the audience was enamored, given her soothing, natural voice tone and a gracious welcome.

"Such a crowd! I am humbled *and* excited in the same moment. Can you believe the angels are already here?"

Deta swept her arms fully, left to right then upward. Then she bent down gracefully to touch the stage floor—palms down. "Thank you, angels. Thank you for reminding me and everyone present that you are *always* here. Just ask!"

Roland was watching from the side of the stage curtain. Deta was authentic. No melodrama, but a gifted person who touched a golden chord in everyone's being.

The way Deta moved, spoke, and aroused everyone in a matter of seconds? Just happened naturally. Sometimes, Roland found himself wondering. Deta truly embodied an earthly and an ethereal angel wherever she presented.

"I want each and every one of you to feel a presence of the angels, your guardians and the archangels. I want each of you to trust this essence of nirvana. Not just today, but each day, every week, and the months ahead, especially as you request and permit their angelic guidance and protection."

There were Deta's earth angels at all events. She made certain that these kindred persons with cordless microphones floated purposefully around the entire auditorium. Deta wanted the incredible potpourri of experiences to be shared, heralded, and celebrated at each event.

"Close your gifted eyes as you sit, very comfy in your cushioned chairs. Let your humble feet stay grounded, flat on the floor. Let your open hands rest upon the top of your thighs. Relax and know that the angels are listening, as they are indeed attentive, light-filled, and so kind. Take three, slow breaths and let your eyelids begin to relax."

Deta was sitting in a comfy chair at center stage when she spoke slowly. Her peaceful eyes were also closed.

"Archangel Michael, come to protect each of us from any worries, the angst, the tumultuous situations, or other negative vibrations. We honor your golden-light sword cutting any ties to these concerns. Our gratitude, Archangel Michael."

Deta continued the meditative, honoring moments. She requested Jophiel's angelic guidance and a heartfelt presence. Deta asked for an intimate space for that golden aura, imprinted images, and the revered signs for today's participants.

Guardian angels of loved ones who passed on and archangels like Raphael, Chamuel, Uriel, Ariel, Gabriel, Metatron, Sandalphon, and other ethereal spirits were summoned. After their introspective session, Deta posed a question.

"Did anyone witness or experience any poignant message, a memorable color, or a symbolic sign?" Deta gazed, touched her heart, and then pointed to the mid-center section for her earth angels with the microphones.

"I am Amanda from our serene Red River, New Mexico. I saw what I would call a radiant peace wall with the exquisite rainbow colors, much like our seven chakras. Such an *inner* peace," the petite woman intoned softly, as she gave a peace sign with the hand-delivered microphone.

"Amanda! Loving, so loving to have all of that energy flooding, releasing, and uniting your inner stillness with a soul-filled synchrony!" Deta offered.

Two men at the top of the center section stood up and spoke melodically. "Up here! Near the angelic spirits." As another earth angel bounded up the aisle and handed the mic to one man, both of them hovered together and spoke in delightful cadences.

"Maurice and Francesco from the Big Apple. Ah, New York. *Love*."

"Both of us heard *love*. Both of us witnessed a lush pink, abstract heart that was floating!"

"Now, that is beautiful. Maurice and Francesco—Equals! Both in sync with your innermost messages and the lush imagery. Each of us can perceive a texture, like a floating heart, enfolding into a color or the hues. You even received the messages. Both of you affirmed that profound beauty," Deta exclaimed, exuding her authentic passion in the company of an infectious smile.

The afternoon event became an immersion—of a hope over despair, our potential over any dismissal, and the possibility over an angst or the compulsive worries.

Roland was Deta's agent, but was also an earnest participant, even from back stage. He always chose to move a chair close to a side curtain of these engaging sessions.

Deta appreciated his choice and let him know at each event. She knew Roland was a soulful agent from the moment that she met him. Now, it was today's moment to savor. Deta's moment of moments—with an enchanting and a memorable closure that was spontaneous.

"Let me offer my gratitude to each of you *and* being present to entrust our day. This afternoon is a novel beginning of a daily commitment with your angelic whisperers and the messages or signs. Angelic realms are replete with an unconditional love for us."

Deta paused purposefully. Then she strolled to the center-front stage and made a sweeping, inclusive gesture to today's audience of kindred spirits.

"Do not create an angst, the anxieties, or any ego worries about the exact minutes that you choose each day. Let an archangel cut any of those chords, if they pop up. Just connect with a self-love and that splendid gratitude. Let the priceless minutes of any striking images, the distinctive hues, meaningful scenarios or phrases, and the resonant feelings take your breath away." Deta paused for a few seconds.

"Let our engaging minutes linger in your enamored hearts. Once any of us is guided, we want to reciprocate and give back to humanity. I remain so grateful for today, my kindred souls."

Facilitators of the angelic realms and learnings from England,

Today, paid forward with another gifted messenger named Deta,

The acknowledgment, acceptance, and practice morph into a multitude...

Simplify

Jacques reflected upon the lifetime choices during his seek-and-find pathways. Anticipation, a confidence, and the intrinsic desires were his personal choices. Angst, a desperation, the fears, and his non-stop worries were the other choices that Jacques owned as well.

This mix of choices was surreal on certain days. Today, Jacques pulled his right hand out of a denim pocket, letting it rest upon his aching, tender heart. Then Jacques lowered his eyes, closing them for at least five minutes.

This year was a series of ramped-up struggles, the horrific clashes, and the weekly trials at home. Today, Jacques elected to embrace any chances for an overdue optimism.

Jacques shocked himself. He started to mumble slowly in today's moment of choice. "Grant the permission and a new release for my possibility and my potential. I choose this hope over my daily despair and hopelessness."

In that instance, something else—timeless or seamless—nestled closer to his nagging, tender heart. Jacques murmured the inner messages that made his aching, a melancholy, and the anguish start to diminish.

Quiet interventions, but a quiet certainty is also present. Today is like a world overriding my surreal world. Earnest. Attentive. Loyal. Caring and compassionate.

This world is like a flowing river of my blessings, particularly on this day. I surrender all of my surreal experiences during this past year and longer.

I am present with the natural, miraculous flow of today. Now, there is just one word that I really need to embrace for my healing heart.

Simplify...

Jacques let a hand rest for several minutes, upon his aching heart,

Struggles at home, horrendous clashes with siblings, and the incessant worries—diminishing with today's hope over those despairs,

His dog-eared pages of a journal were tossed aside, as Jacques penned today's entry with one word. Simplify...

Awakened Cemetery

Evangeline was doing her walkabout in the cemetery. She admitted, "A lot of people in this town think I am weird for walking every day in the old cemetery."

She giggled, wondering what sensational, theatrical stories were floating around the town. Perhaps, there was even an exotic tale that people suspected or imagined.

"No need to fret. I am fond of you, dearest ole' cemetery. Your namesakes on these historic gravestones, now the symbolic souls, are still precious. I am gifted with the inner messages," Evangeline whispered, as she walked by Abigail and Hortense. The rose stone quartz with a green Italian patina was simple, an elegant tribute to their long union and a legacy.

Today brought forth the dramatic, whirling winds and a chill factor, but Evangeline dressed in her warmest hiking boots and leggings underneath her purple-passion jeans with the whimsical patchwork. A thermal top and sweater, a long fax-fur coat nicknamed "don't mess with me, I'm Big Bear," and her cuddly, felt-lined mittens were super. Best of all, Evangeline chose her mother's favorite and styling Celtic hat.

She picked up her pace and turned against the intermittent wind gusts. Evangeline yanked her fax-fur hood over the Celtic hat when she arrived at the pristine lake and hillside with the children. Evangeline was unaware when he approached the section with these children's gravestones.

"Quite beautiful and touching," he commented, reaching to tie his scarf a bit tighter around his hoodie for the next wind gust. "It is a lovely hillside for these precious children."

"Oh my, I just realized that you walked up. Had to be a wind gust and my bigger-than-life hoodie," Evangeline replied, with her raspy, louder voice.

He smiled. "My older sister is here. I shall meet her on the other side," he offered, without any reservation. "Oh, my belief, if I offended you with such candor."

"Not at all! My oldest brother is not in this cemetery, but in another town where I grew up. My mother carried to term, a stillborn boy who they named after my Dad. Even as a young child, I told my parents that I would met him in heaven one day. I always remember," Evangeline declared, in a tender, genial voice.

"Well, I guess I met a kindred friend in this town. Seems to be another blessing," he mused, loud enough to be heard between the next wind gust. He held out a leather-gloved hand and grinned. "Hi there, I am Shane."

"Nice to meet you, Shane. I am Evangeline," she replied, with a pleasant smile and an outstretched, hand-knit mitten.

"I think that I heard a neighbor mention that name and your recent arrival in our town. Yes, I am certain, now that I reflect. Honestly, I was curious. Well, no longer!" Shane continued, in an appealing voice with a charming grin.

"I walk here daily, but our paths did not cross until Mother Nature's winds of time intended us to meet," Shane offered, looking at her fabulous eyes and an engaging smile again.

"I like that—an intention—paths meant to cross with the winds of time," Evangeline stated spontaneously.

"Well, Evangeline, it might seem a bit forward, but the sunset and another wind gust are prompting me to ask. And, I must confess—my curiosity about Evangeline, our new resident. Could I buy you a cup of coffee at our famous local diner?" Shane requested, with an infectious grin.

"Not too forward at all! My colder toes are talking and convincing me that a bold roast coffee and our continued visit are stellar ideas!" Evangeline declared, giving a few girlish giggles this time.

Off they walked at a brisk pace, out of the ole' cemetery towards the town center with the famous diner. Mother Nature's winds of time and their kindred spirit with a chance meeting were an unforeseen destiny.

"Hi Celeste, could you perk up that famous, bold-roast coffee for two hikers in desperate need?" Shane asked, giving her a hug. Before answering, Celeste glanced quickly at Evangeline.

"Sure thing, Shane! Glad to see that you brought our new resident. Our town diner is a gem, an eclectic haven that she needed to experience, eh?"

"Exactly! Great choice of words to describe you...and, of course, our famous diner."

"Celeste, I gather that I am about to experience *the epicenter* of town. Looking forward to this experience," proclaimed Evangeline, pulling off her mittens and extending her graceful hand with a firm handshake.

Her treasured Larimar ring from her mother was spotted immediately. "Oh, a favorite keepsake from my mother," Evangeline added, rubbing the gem affectionately.

"My word, I have not seen a Larimar beauty like your ring. Is it possible that your mother or both of you traveled to the Dominican Republic for this revered gem?"

"Why, yes! Celeste, we took a spectacular mother-daughter trip to Punta Cana. We went horseback riding in the breathtaking countryside, took excursions to two villages, and Mom even did a zip line. What precious memories, especially since she died last year of colon cancer," Evangeline intoned gently, pausing purposefully when she rubbed the Larimar ring again.

"So sorry, Evangeline. I was caught up in the stunning beauty of your Larimar gem and its ring-setting."

"Oh, I keep my Mom close to my heart. I would not wish anyone to suffer as my precious Mom did that last year. I appreciate that you noticed and knew quite a bit about my beloved keepsake, Celeste!"

"I traveled to Punta Cana as well. Seems that we own an exquisite imagery and the lovely memories from their countryside, smaller villages, and the pristine waters. I am also sorry for your loss, but uplifted by your mother-daughter travels and the last adventures," added Shane, looking straight into Evangeline's misty eyes. Shane touched her hand lightly, with a momentary caress over her Larimar ring.

"Both of you are kind-hearted and appreciative. Now, let us toast to this eclectic diner and my new-found friends with our bold-roast coffee. Plus, the warmth and an obvious empathy that each of you extended to me!"

Celeste scooted away for the bold-roast coffee. Shane took Evangeline's hand and headed to a small table near the window, pulling up another chair for Celeste.

All of them lifted the steaming mugs for a cha-ching click. Their laughter and visiting added to the blissful day. Shane accompanied Evangeline to her log cabin. It was nestled in a couple acres at the edge of the town center.

"You bought the best deal in town, you know. This was my uncle's homestead for the last seven years. What a fun and caring man who touted his saying, 'I'm gonna really live LIFE!' My endearing uncle died in his sleep, but not until he had lived a loving-kind and an adventurous life!" Shane expressed, with such enthusiasm and a transparent love.

He stopped at the front entry and smiled. Shane was about to speak about their chance meeting and a very pleasant afternoon when Evangeline gave him a hug.

"Thank you so much, Shane. Today was unexpected—our chance meeting on the whirling dervish day, such fun, and the inspirational visits. The *epicenter* for this town, meeting Celeste, and the eclectic town diner were authentic. I am full to the brim—joyful and ever so grateful!"

"First, let me return that grand hug. Now, listen carefully," Shane murmured, holding her shoulders gently. "Chance meeting? I think that both of us *awakened* the cemetery. Perhaps, we awakened the guardian whisperers? I truly believe that kindred and like-minded individuals cross paths in the unexpected moments. Like a spiral labyrinth walk! What do you sense or know in your vibrant and unique heart at this very moment?" Shane asked softly, while gazing into Evangeline's serene eyes.

AT REST

The AT REST cemetery and her nature walkabouts,

Reminders of the past, a present, and the symbolic future,

Evangeline was looking up and letting go, taken off guard when Shane appeared,

Intersecting paths, like a spiral labyrinth walk, meant to be...

Gaze Upward

Mahalia and Claudio delighted and doted upon the small island of Boracay. Its powdery white sand, an abundance of tropical flora, and the untainted shorelines were a godsend. In one hour, they would fly from Manila for another stunning reprieve.

Filipinos and avid travelers touted a certain purity in Boracay. This diminutive island tendered a calm interlude, a refreshing hiatus, or an engaging night life in the Philippines.

Mahalia and Claudio created a quality time for their frequent rejuvenation. They strolled and jogged the beach shorelines that showcased the crystal-azure waters.

Mahalia would sprint for a mile, pause for several minutes, and gaze upward. She would motion to Claudio.

"Remember? We always pause to take in whatever keepsakes happen in our day," Mahalia pronounced boldly, with a loving glance and her arresting smile.

"Absolutely! I shall never take such a bestowal for granted. Our sky artistry uplifts us. The spectrum of colors invites our genuine re-awakening, a different way of gazing and anticipating," Claudio whispered in Mahalia's ear. Both of them intertwined their arms affectionately and gazed upward.

"The unknown, like an idyllic dance of the innocences, begins to unfold as today's clouds transform," Mahalia affirmed. Their intensified heartbeats became a synchronicity with each stroll and their intermittent sprints. Today's keepsakes—their devout gratitude, a fortuitous love, and their peace were immeasurable.

Jog another mile, pause again, intertwine adoringly, and gaze upward from a white-powdery shoreline and the crystal-azure water. A new cloud formation revealed an unforgettable imagery, their authentic enlightenment. Something happened in this exact moment that Mahalia and Claudio gazed upward.

"Claudio, you know what? Right now, I just knew! I shall not have any more miscarriages," Mahalia declared.

Claudio nodded, kissing her tenderly. His hand-clasp enfolded her slender fingers as they waded together. They hugged in the crystal-azure water and gentle waves, releasing an ebb and flow of their salty, appreciative tears.

Kindred islanders were privy to this phenomenon of pausing, gazing upward, and just knowing. The inevitable—a dance of the innocences—would be forthcoming.

These soul-filled moments unveiled what Mahalia and Claudio were supposed to remember. Begin anew.

Dance of the innocences is forthcoming,

Unveiling what Mahalia and Claudio needed to remember,

Begin anew…

Never Forgetting

Emma, Nigel, and Cyrus drove together to a compelling and esoteric drumming circle. Each week, this sacred space and a mystic quality of time, reaffirmed an individualistic, the collaborative, and a quantum truth.

Emma was the epitome of her namesake and its Germanic origin. She exuded the bona fide and undeniable meanings, namely a wholeness and a universality. Nigel, like his namesake of Irish and Gaelic origins, manifested an essence and the contagious attitude of a champion. Cyrus was akin to his namesake and its Persian origin. He emanated a brightness of the sun, a sentient person who bestowed an ultimate caring.

"Let us not forget. Let us receive and release. Drumming brings us back. We harken from a soul. Someday, each of us will return to our soul," they said, in tandem. Clasped hands with a firm squeeze and a release began their rhythmic drumming.

Each person in their sacred circle had read appealing metaphysical books and savored the plentiful insights. Whenever a darkness started to invade a space of living, there were their authentic endeavors to release completely. Each individual searched and discovered a light to illuminate an alternate pathway.

Emma, Nigel, and Cyrus met initially at a drumming circle during a regional conference. That evening, they enjoyed a lakeside bonfire and talked for a fascinating two hours. No coincidence that each of them lived in the same state and a neighboring community.

"You want to seek out or start a drumming circle in our area?" they posed, almost in unison, before the end of that magnificent evening of dialogues and their departures. The multitude of phone calls sealed their mutual wish for a long-term and a like-minded friendship.

Emma read and reviewed certain contemporary books, sharing a nitty-gritty of the rich contexts. These profound rites of passage heightened an authenticity of being and becoming. Cyrus and Nigel adopted the compelling narrative of Emma's vibrant passages that she composed.

Emma read her narratives. Then she let the penned thinking moments complete her day or week.

Dare to move forward to a new healing place, a sacred world. Trust the offering of possibility or a protection rather than the past, any present burdens, or the envisioned limitations.

Turn on the light again…and again. Cross over the perceived boundaries that dismiss the potential of a dream, a hope, a vision, or a different tomorrow for Mother Earth. Celebrate the sacred hoops within your dreamscapes. Receive this protection.

There were no dismissals or the denials. The trio accepted, practiced, and intensified the sacred rites of passage. They discerned and appreciated that an unexpected gift of their cherished friendship became a favored destiny.

A decade later? Not to be forgotten.

Emma, Nigel, and Cyrus never strayed from this valued kinship of a decade. They chose purposefully and attentively. They cherished a kindred spirit, revering their sacred drumming circle.

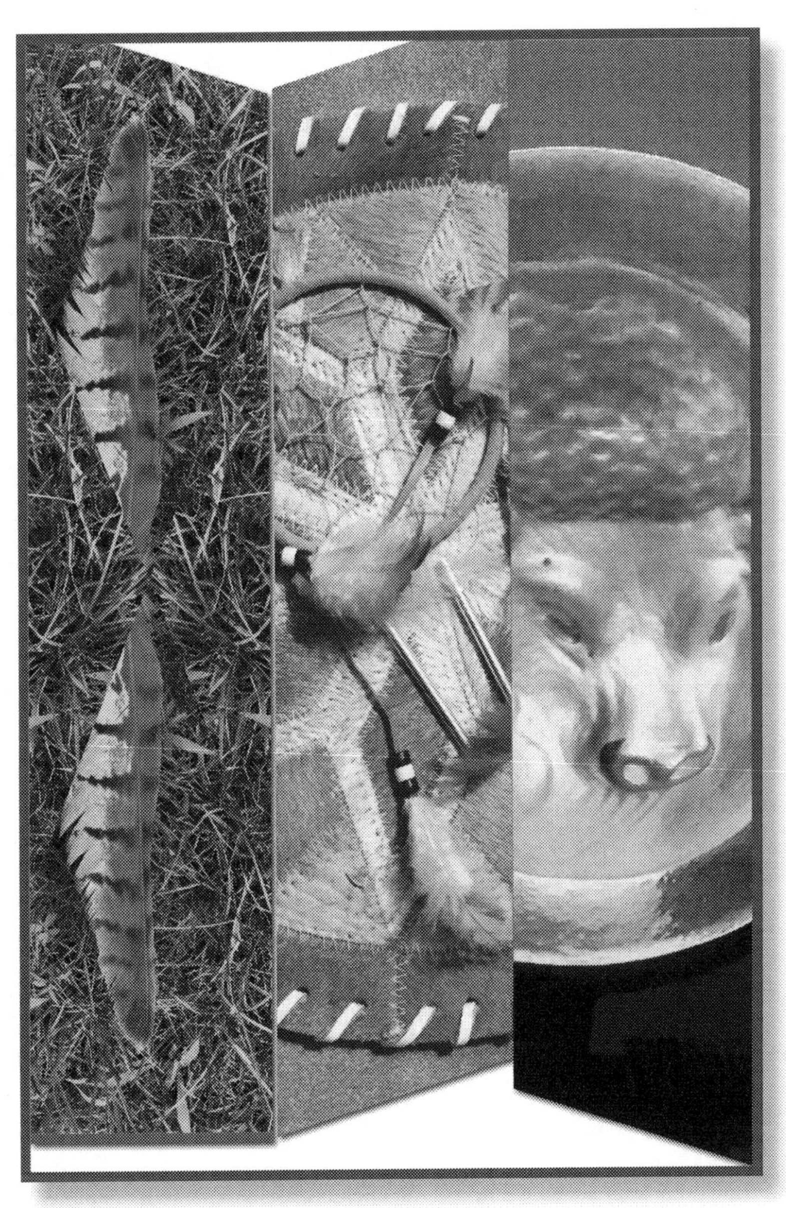

Drumming circles and the rhythms unite Emma, Nigel, and Cyrus,

The sacred four corners of our Mother Earth,

The sacred hoops of a dreamscape and an inherent protection,

With a reverence, they never forgot...

Wanton Stillness

Seiko basked in a soft repose, enthralled with this early morning and the light silhouettes. She inhaled the cleansing air, honoring a sea mist upon her elegant cheeks, sparkling eyes, and pink lips. Seiko looked forward to these spring sojourns in La Jolla, the rugged coastline of this seaside community and the exceptional Torrey Pines State National Reserve in San Diego.

Seiko gave a longer release with the multiple breaths, her exhalations inviting an intimate harmony and an ardent commitment. These moments brought forth a wanton stillness. Atop this vista on the rugged coastline, Seiko spoke like her Japanese name—of the serene truths, stalwart accomplishments, and her innate vitality.

"Trust. Travel beyond my struggles," Seiko uttered, in a chant-like voice. Seiko paused briefly, letting the intoxicating sea mist refresh her.

"Know myself. Important to renew these truths, stay acquainted with thyself," she whispered. Seiko ended with an inspirational closure after her three, deeper breaths.

"Billions of new brain cells for our mind, body, and spirit. They complete each day, Seiko. Valued gifts. Experience and sense a creative dawning, a sunrise glory. Receive and give back," Seiko murmured. These affirmations, like her Japanese heritage, became today's innate vitality.

Seiko believed passionately about the known and the unknown dimensions during a lifespan. She honored her strong Asian womanhood, promoting a deserving justice and an attitude of empowerment for all Asian women.

Seiko reached for a rainbow-colored pen, a gift from her revered Reiki master. Today, she scripted the first-rate and the rare moments.

"La Jolla and Torrey Pines create a stronger presence. Today's unveiling becomes my legacy of an improved consciousness. Pursue and maintain my self-care and the self-love," Seiko penned, stopping to reread the inscriptions in her golden-etched notebook.

Seiko respected this circadian rhythm with her heartbeats, both in Japan and in the United States. She remained atop the cliffside vista, bowing her head to pay homage to today's wanton stillness.

Seiko cherished these tranquil locales for her yearly sojourn in the United States. Each spring, La Jolla and Torrey Pines offered a unique imprinting.

These mindful reprieves reaffirmed Seiko's innate appreciation of the priority and personal relevance of self-love and self-care. Then Seiko was better able to enhance a fervent compassion and her intensity for our worldly and spiritual connections.

Seiko departed each spring with a delicate, cultivated realm of stillness and an exclusive thanksgiving. The ultimate endowment was a wanton desire to savor the illustrious seconds, precious minutes, and indelible hours in her life journey.

"I am a stronger, Asian woman. I shall honor my self-promises," Seiko murmured, bowing in the sea mist winds of time.

A towering eagle, manifesting Seiko's unconditional love for Japan and the United States,

Endowments from the La Jolla and Torrey Pines sojourns and a wanton stillness with each visit,

Transformative minutes, hours, and days to infuse Seiko's intentions for our worldly, peaceful, and respectful life journeys...

Untie The Ribbon

"Have you untied the ribbon with today's gift? Today, tomorrow, and even next week, look forward to untying each ribbon," the professor expressed compassionately.

She observed the classroom to see if anyone wished to respond. "Oh, wondrous! Go ahead, Catalina."

"I untied my ribbon and opened today's gift, a ball of red-earthen clay. I sculpted an angel, cupping her in my blissful, blessed hands. Then I closed my eyes, imagining and recapturing my creation."

"Your gift is stunning and provocative. Did anything happen this morning or in the afternoon, Catalina?"

"My day became full of thoughts, revealing a symmetry of our world and the importance of harmony in our different relationships. I think my angel bequeathed another bounty—the rest of my subliminal, untapped beauty with a *new* friend." Catalina's face was full of rapture, especially as she gazed into the peaceful eyes of her professor.

"What an evolution to untie today's ribbon, to receive, to create, and then—to receive another subliminal beauty, Catalina. Thank you for conveying the entirety."

"Juan, you look like you might want to share? If so, please feel free to indulge us with your untie-the-ribbon gift of today."

"I do want to share, Professor Chamuel! I asked for my guardian angel, my younger sister who died last year in a car accident, to please give me a sign. As I walked to class, I knew in a few seconds. Look up. I saw wispy clouds and the golden sun with a pink ray. My dear sister loved pink EVERYTHING!"

"You knew to look up, Juan. Very perceptive! Class, do you remember our articles? We read anecdotes about the loving communiques with our earthly family or significant friends. There is a soothing sense or a sign. So we talk—aloud or within—to our loved ones who have passed on," Professor Chamuel repeated, in an amicable cadence. "Other inspirational experiences and your personal insights?"

The class kept sharing today's gifts, the symbolic ribbons that they chose to untie. Professor Chamuel always encouraged the dialogues and created a class climate for a conscious caring, the honesty, and the non-judgements. She ended today's class with one of her quintessential insights.

"Whenever there is a sense of guardian angels or the archangels, an inner solace or a peace arrives. Believe and entrust this angelic guidance in the special moments of synchrony and their adulation. Thank all of you for untying your ribbons. Each of you deserve and is worthy of today's gift."

As the students left class, Dr. Chamuel put a hand over her heart, an affirmation that she would never lose a passion for teaching and this unique gift of reciprocal learning. Many students were watching and head-nodding with her heart gesture. They followed suit, as they departed from the classroom.

Their class ended before the sunset. As different groups of students walked outside, they glanced upward. Several of them gasped and pointed up to the sky.

A brief rain happened during their indoor class. An emergence of the late afternoon sunbeams created a breathtaking rainbow.

Before sunset, Mother Nature had untied another ribbon for all of them, a gifting of this sky art.

Catalina and Juan untied their ribbons for the subliminal beauty,

Professor Chamuel encouraged her students to receive and accept,

Each day, a majestic surprise and a nourishing gift were imminent...

Life

She was an ingenious and masterly teacher. Christina opened her online writing class with today's brainstorm and a touch of whimsy.

"Write faster than the speed of light," she encouraged. "Let your fingerlings fly across a journal or the notepad, writing beyond measure. Or type like a feisty, wild woman or a fiery, spunky man. Imagine your fingers levitating, almost taking flight off your computer keyboard!"

The students were ready to skyrocket. So was Christina. Next came the writing prompt that would touch their IQ and EQ. Christina never ceased to be amazed at what happened whenever the IQ, our intellectual gray matter, morphed with the EQ, our heart synapses and neurons. A unique phenomena—just knowing—happened swiftly.

"In a precious second, this is what life does…" Christina spoke calmly. "Snafu fifteen minutes with this inviting prompt. Oh yes, each of you can write faster than the speed of light," she declared, speaking melodically to coax them.

Tara began. Her fingerlings flew across the page, a purple pen scribbling and scrawling across the salmon, lavender, and light green sheets of paper.

In a precious second, this is what life does… Life brings you a bonus, the remarkable gift each day. Just untie the bow, the string, or the glossy ribbon. Reach down to touch something meant just for you. Closed eyes. Surprise yourself as you draw out whatever your heart really craves or needs today. Be free, love passionately, run to the stars, hold a lover tighter…

Lorenzo paused and repeated Christina's writing prompt. He chose to type on his favorite laptop, envisioning his fingers flying across the keyboard.

In a precious second, this is what life does… It whizzes past you, if you do not pay attention. Be vigilant and become immersed in the world around you. Today, I caught sight of a homeless man in an abandoned store entry, as I walked toward a downtown convenience store.

I bought two cups of soup, one for myself and the other cup for the homeless man without a name. As I hastened back to that store entry, he had rolled over on tattered, seedy blanket. I bent down and told him I had soup to share.

He did not move. I wondered and worried. Maybe he had died? Then he groaned and rolled over, almost onto my feet.

This homeless man had beautiful blue eyes, wizened skin, and smelled foul to my nostrils. I handed him a spoon, then the soup.

He threw the spoon at my chest, took the soup, and drank it in his wobbly hands. He stopped and glared at my eyes.

I took my soup, showed him, and left it next to him. He grabbed my arm hard, growled a few words I could not understand.

*He growled again, leaning closer. I was "a f****** prick."*

I still left my soup…

Christina was also writing, exuding a feisty look and the weird chuckles. Her students liked that she chose to write ASAP, right along with them. Their online Zoom classes were an intriguing experience. At least they would meet their classmates during the classes and whenever they wanted to dialogue.

Christina encouraged them again. "Fifteen minutes! Share your crazy, just write, zig zag, spontaneous phrases or paragraphs—all become your phenomenal stories!"

The university offered more classes online, only a few classes on the main campus. Over the years, Christina adapted well. However, she preferred the bliss and a natural high, whenever the campus classes happened.

During today's fifteen minutes and that writing prompt, Christina scribbled on a pad of lavender paper. Sharing her writings with the students became a ritual, the anticipative moments for her students. She read the scribbles, a last-second title of "Christina's composting."

In a precious second, this is what life does… It surprises you when it creeps up all of a sudden like a whirling dervish, a spinning top where all the colors blend so fast. Outside the windows of my bungalow, the wind whispers hold my secrets, if I want to listen, listen, and listen.

Do I hear what is meant for me today in my bending birch and pine trees, their nods to the universe, perhaps the gods and goddesses somewhere out there? Am I afraid to hear? Am I courageous enough to listen closely?

Enough means I shall try and try again to be attentive. Maybe if I cup my hands gently around my right and left ears, I shall hear a few inklings or an innuendo of the sage messages meant for me.

I am waiting patiently to become that wiser soul…

By the end of class, several students had read their crazy, zig zag, and phenomenal writings. Christina reread today's writing, a frequent request. No great mystique why she felt a real bliss from these Zoom classes.

"I am proud and humbled that each of you elects to stay in the moment, not worrying about perfecting your zig zag writings. We are often conditioned to critique, thinking that our best writings will emerge. Maybe so? Maybe not? Zig zag writings can surprise you, especially if you continue the experience.

"I surprise myself, even after many years of teaching." Christina paused intentionally, before ending today's writing class.

"Life is a journey. Our vibrant classes affirm that truth. Thanks, my feisty and enraptured students, for that valued reminder. Until our next on-cloud-nine class, try another zig zag writing!"

Free spirits let loose, teetering on writing paths never envisioned,

Grab the gusto, welcoming the tremors of lightning-bolt stories,

Like the dolphins, not knowing where or when, but traveling way out yonder...

Epilogue

Everyone owns a story. Jubilee memoirs, a questionable year, the inevitable regrets, the resonant sounds of exquisite merriment, or certain sorrows greet us.

In this life space of drifting and wayfaring, there are countless passages—our roads travelled or not. Is there a yearning to write down these personal memoirs before they become foggy? Or perhaps, become lost in the deeper recesses of our mind-caverns?

Each of us greets a muse or two when we recapture a story in our lifespan. Real events that happen in a special year. Different or memorable relationships that come to our mind and heart. The peaks and valleys of our personal journey that permit us to stretch, like it or not.

The authentic characters and the vivid scenes replay in our mind and heart. Come hither, our diminishing or vibrant stories with the lasting images and memories.

Let a free spirit move your hand across the next blank pages. Use this granting of a special space and whatever time, day, or month to pen a real story in your journey, a wayfaring that you own.

My first story of receiving and accepting, a memoir that I own...

Everyone owns another story or two, the *fiction* stories. We witness the diverse personas entering and perhaps, exiting our life journey. Leftover impressions and our reflections seem to meld together across the years. Stories evolve.

In a given day or week, there is an inclination to recall a myriad of our impressions. Like a time tunnel, there are bits and pieces—a unique concoction—that morphs into a cast of distinctive characters propelled into life-altering situations. The journeys happen.

When there is an inner urgency to pause, pursue, and capture our fictional story, something clicks or sparks in that colorful, bizarre, or alluring moment. Our imagination does the trick, as a novel beginning of our potential ideas, a realm of possibilities, and the captive or our cliffhanger endings come forth.

Let this free spirit move your hand across the forthcoming blank pages. Add the additional pages or choose to compose on your computer. Whatever amount of space or time, let your fictional storylines run their gamut.

Let your energy ebb and flow into the unexpected passages. Witness. Imagine. Envision. Permit a flash fiction or a short story to emerge with your creative writing.

My hand flows in the moment, as I create an imaginative first story...

My hand flows in the moment, as I create an imaginative second story...

LIFE IS
BEAUTIFUL

Like the wild horse, my innate courage is seized,

is accepted,

is beautiful.

Like a rare Lady Slipper floral, my free spirit is witnessed,

is accepted,

is beautiful.